INITIATION
The Initiation of Catherine Rei

PETE SEARS

VOLUME ONE IN THE CATHERINE REI QUARTET

The beginning of the sexual adventures of a previously dissatisfied young woman. Introduced to the mysterious Forum, Catherine Rei finds herself becoming addicted to the dark pleasures of multiple sexual partners and bondage.

"A graphically beautiful erotic odyssey."

The Initiation of Catherine Rei
The Obedience of Catherine Rei
The Progression of Catherine Rei
The Revelation of Catherine Rei

I0557779

APS BOOKS
Stourbridge

APS Books
The Stables,
Aberford,
West Midlands,
LS25 3AE

APS Books is a subsidiary of
the APS Publications imprint

www.andrewsparke.com

1 ~ FIRST ARRIVAL

Catherine Rei finds herself ushered into a grand ante-chamber.

"Wait here for instructions."

She sinks into a plush settee. Burgundy velvet. Extremely comfortable but disconcertingly low. She can see it'll be a struggle to get to her feet again and wonders if she should stand up now. Perhaps use one of the wooden chairs set out in the window bay. But she doesn't for fear someone will come back in, catching her in mid-manoeuvre. She compensates, straightening her back and tugging her skirt down over her thighs. Folding her hands in her lap.

Catherine Rei is now still, watching the progress of the hands of the antique French clock on the mantelpiece. It chimes for the quarter hour and the minutes pass. Twenty. Twenty-one. Twenty-two.

The double doors are opened without warning and two men enter. The first is the servant who opened the front door when she rang the bell and ushered her into this room. Behind him stalks an unusually tall man to whom the butler now bows and then disappears. Catherine Rei makes to get up but is told to stay where she is.
"Don't look at me. Keep your eyes on the carpet. Don't pay any heed to whatever I do."

Catherine Rei doesn't know if she should utter agreement. Decides she isn't required to speak. Stays silent. She's conscious of the presence behind her but it still startles her when unseen hands float a black silk scarf before her, twirling it into the perfect shape to cover her eyes, knotting it carefully in place to serve as a highly effective blindfold. She can't help herself. Gives a little gasp, quickly stifled.

A moment later and hands take her elbows, coaxing her to rise smoothly from the depths of the cushions in which she lounges.

"Come through with me." She is guided across the room. Her progress is stopped in the doorway. And the man speaks again. "I'll warn you when you get there, but there'll be a step up to a seat for you. Sit down and compose yourself. When you're ready the Master will ask you some questions. Speak clearly. And truthfully. If you lie, we will know and the game will be over for you. Anything you are asked to do, you will do without hesitation but nothing more. If in doubt do nothing and the instruction will be repeated or clarified. We have to be sure of you and there may be other days, other sessions like this before you move to the next level. Do you understand?"

"Yes." Catherine Rei's voice is soft but clear. Unconsciously she uses her free hand to smooth her hair. She nods. "I'm ready." And moves forward into whatever awaits her. Awaits her mind and her body.

2 ~ COMMITMENT

The scene awaiting Catherine Rei is lushly staged. Even if she can't see it. Rich drapes and tall ladder-backed chairs, well upholstered for comfort.

Catherine manages not to pause in the doorway. Moving forward blindfolded into this inner chamber, a hand firmly in place on her forearm to lead her to her appointed place.

"Up. One step. Turn round. Sit."

She does exactly as she's told and the hand guides her into the uncushioned chair on its dais at the exact centre of the room. A silence settles. And lasts longer than anyone in Catherine's position could find remotely comfortable. But she dare say nothing.

A harsh male clearing of the throat and a deep voice gives Catherine her next instruction. "State your full name."

"Catherine Joyce Rei."

"And are you here of your own volition?"

"I am."

"And do you consent to all that will be done to you here?"

Catherine hesitates. She doesn't have a clue where giving full consent will lead. But she knows if she doesn't give it, her adventure will end right here and now. In consequence she keeps her voice low-pitched. Under tight control. "Yes."

"Thank you, Catherine. In return the assurance you now receive is that nobody here will truly harm you. You are hereby granted safe passage in this company. And if you are brought too close to the brink of what you can bear you need only utter one simple phrase. *I beg you, Master.* Do you understand?"

Catherine nods.

"Please speak out."

"Yes. I…I understand."

"Good. Then I declare the Forum in session. Who has the first question for Catherine?"

"I do." A lighter voice. Not the tall man from the ante-room. "Catherine. Tell us why you think you're here."

She sucks in a deep breath. Tries to hold herself together. "Well…A girlfriend, Barbara, told me about her experience and the release it brought her." Easier to say it now she's started. Into her pre-prepared answer. "I've had men. But it's always been disappointing. I want to feel so much more."

"Always?" Do you mean always, Catherine?"

"Well not always. There was…a long time ago."

The Master smoothly intervenes. "We'll be exploring your early sexual history on another occasion. For now it's enough that you seek another form of satisfaction. Is that the truth, Catherine?"

"Yes."

"And what will you do? What will you allow to be done in pursuit of this … satisfaction?"

"Anything you want of me." A formulaic answer she's learned from Barbara but it has the desired effect. A low hum of approval around the room, telling her heightened senses that there are at least half a dozen people here with her.

"Well said." Abruptly the tone changes. No longer gentle. "Spread your legs".

Catherine tries to respond without thinking about the command.

"Quickly." And stay in the chair".

She edges her bottom forward and wriggles her skirt up a little to give herself more freedom of movement. Her long legs separate as instructed. She knows that, whoever they are, they can see her panties through the dark mesh of her tights. Can scan her shapely knees and the soft flesh of her inner thighs above her black stiletto boots. She desperately wants to say something. To solicit verbal acknowledgement of their approval. The silence in the room weighs heavily on her.

The next order comes. "Stand up."

She obeys with too much alacrity. A hand stops her falling down the step at the edge of the dais. "Be careful." It's the tall man. She takes half a pace back. Straightens her back and her skirt drops back down into place just above her knees.

"One thing. Next time you wear stockings not pantyhose". She hears the instruction and a rising tide of relief hits her. Whatever the terms of her test, she's passed it. They want her to return. The hand is back on her arm and she's heading for the door again.

"Here next Wednesday at eight pm. Don't be late. Now bring in our next piece of business."

Catherine walks out bravely, head held high. Despite the blindfold. What they don't know is that inside she's reviewing all that she's discovered. And in particular that she's learned something unexpected about the Master. He speaks perfect English but English isn't his language of birth. And wherever he learned to speak it was from an American tutor. The accent is there to be heard and he didn't comment on her tights. He used a yankee word. Pantyhose. She can't help grinning. Information, like sex itself, is power.

3 ~ BOUND TO PLEASE

A week passes slowly for Catherine Rei. Work. The gym. Shopping. An evening in a bar with Barbara, who won't answer any questions about the Forum. A night child-minding for her sister. Nothing helps the time go by save at a snail's pace.

Nevertheless seven days do pass and eventually she finds herself once more outside the large Georgian house in town. Dressed almost as before but, in accordance with the Master's instructions, with one essential difference. A difference which somehow both increases her rising excitement and adds to her sense of vulnerability.

This time the blindfold is applied directly on arrival. In the hall. By the tall man. And instead of being ushered into the ante-chamber to the left or into the large room to which she was taken for her initial questioning, she's coerced with a hand in the small of her back to climb the broad flight of stairs and to enter somewhere which feels to her smaller. More intimate. And carpeted underfoot. Her escort asks her to turn round. When she obeys, he gives her a little push. The backs of her knees make contact with a low divan. "Don't resist." She feels his hand touch her breast. Briefly. And then he pushes her again, with a little more force and she sprawls backwards onto the bed.

His next move is to take her right wrist and place around it a loop of soft material which he tightens until she couldn't slip it off even if she wanted to. But she doesn't wish to struggle. Especially as she feels his mouth touching her, softly kissing her pulse-point. A moment later and her other hand is secured in the same fashion. Again the acknowledging kiss. Catherine shivers. With pleasure.

"You like that then." He sounds pleased at the effect he's having on her. He's not finished either. He takes hold one of her black high-heeled boots, using his free hand to unzip and then remove it. She feels him move away from the bed and there is no plopping noise so he hasn't just carelessly discarded her boot. A moment later and he's tackling the other, taking it off and putting it away. His large hand takes a strong grip on her shapely little ankle, holds her right leg firmly in place while the palm of his other hand slides gently up the length of her leg, past the lacy welt of her stocking-top and caresses the smooth skin of her inner thigh, fleetingly. Suddenly business-like he's securing each leg in turn. Pulling them apart and tying them open. Shortening the bonds holding her arms so her body stretches.

His comment "Very nice." And then he does something she doesn't expect. Her short skirt is up around her waist and he pulls downwards on its hem, covering her panties. She almost wants him to touch her there. Between her legs. She's aware she's leaking wetness. If he touches her he'll find out just how turned on she already is. But he doesn't.

A pillow is nudged under her head and he asks in that deep, concerned tone of his, "Are you comfortable?"

She wants to tell him that the bed is far more supportive than the mattress she sleeps on at home. But she remembers the warning that she must speak only to answer what is said to her. So all she says is a simple "Yes."

"Good."

Catherine feels rather than hears the door softly closing. The displacement of the air not the sound. And her wait begins.

4 ~ ON THE BED

Perhaps she dozes. It doesn't seem to Catherine to be that long before the door to her room is flung open and several people come into the room. But it is in fact over two hours. She stretches her body, flexing it as much as her bonds will allow.

Nobody says a thing. The tension in the room; in Catherine herself; is a living thing, clawing excitedly at her insides. She jumps in alarm as somebody touches her foot.

"Sshhh."

Catherine forces herself to relax. Allows them to stroke her stockinged legs.

Movement. The weight of a body settling on the bed beside her head. Hands running through her hair. More hands moving across her body; undoing her blouse buttons; reaching underneath her back to undo the catch of her bra, lifting the fabric away to give unfettered access to her breasts. She gasps at the first cupping of a breast, a calloused hand cradling her gently, fingers spreading to reach her nipple. Which stiffens with instant arousal. Somebody on her other side now too. A multiplicity of hands coming up her legs and across her chest. Her mouth and her neck being kissed. Not over-gently now but with barely repressed urgency. She can't help herself. Moans with excitement. and a frisson of fear as fingers glide across her flat stomach and down into her panties. Not one hand. Or two. At least three duelling sets of fingers parting her pubic hair and pushing her thighs further apart.

The first words spoken. "Let me sort that." Not aimed at her. Something coldly metallic against the skin of her hip. Her panties gone. Cut away. And there's no longer any impediment to those who are stretching her legs open as much as her velvet bonds will permit. Or to the fingertips testing the resilience of her labia or dipping into the sopping wetness of her pussy. A thumb and forefinger take possession of her clitoris, manipulating the tender area around it. The growing sensations are becoming overwhelming and she can't distinguish the extent to which a well-greased digit is circling her anus, a slow, insistent pressure masked for her by the intensity of touch she's experiencing on every other part of her body.

She could not have known in advance how all-embracing this pleasure would be. She fights it. Is made to fight it by the cunningly aware advances and retreats of pressure on her skin. Is coaxed towards one inevitable end and then not allowed to take it. Groans in joy and frustration. And the feelings grow stronger and stronger.

There are fingers pushing into her. Brushing and re-brushing her inner tissues. Curving up against the front wall of her quim. Touching the knot of sensitive nerves beneath her clitoris, which is still in someone else's grip. The exhilarating and unique sensation of being manhandled from both sides at one and the same time.

Another voice altogether. One which hasn't spoken in her hearing tonight so far at all. The voice with the slight American twang. The Master's voice. "Let her come now."

Catherine doesn't need the fingers moving more urgently against her. His voice; his permission is enough. Her orgasm hits her like a runaway train. Shaking her whole body violently and feverishly. She's unaware of screaming. In another world entirely for the moments in which it seizes and possesses every fragment of her being. She would levitate from the bed if the velvet ropes did not hold her down. She doesn't know what she would do if she was unrestrained. For an age she doesn't know anything at all.

Catherine thinks she dreams. Of being taken by Gods and Goddesses. Of impossible emotions. Of previously unimaginable pleasure. She wakes holding tightly to her pillow, curled up on the soft mattress, released from the constraints which tied her wrists and ankles to the bed and covered against the cool night air by a heavy velour throw.

There's nobody else in her room. She fixes her bra, does up her blouse and gets up gingerly. Her legs, colt-like, seem unused to the act of carrying her weight. Parts of her seem exquisitely tender and she no longer has panties to cover herself. She tugs her skirt as far down as it will go. Finds and slips on her boots. Opens the door, crosses the landing and heads down the magnificent staircase. The whole house is silent. Empty.

In the hall, rising from a chair by the front door, she finds the butler. He has her jacket. Holds it for her to put on. Opens the door for her. "Goodnight, Miss." Nothing ironic in his tone at all.

"Goodnight."

On the street with no other choice she hails a taxi. Goes home to her flat. Wondering if there will be a third Wednesday for her or not.

5 ~ READINESS

Catherine Rei doesn't know if she will ever get used to the uncertainty. She doubts she'll ever learn to have the necessary patience to simply await the call or to let the time pass until her next given appointment. But she has no alternative. She knows if she tries to force the issue or come unbidden to the house, then it will be over. But it's so hard to resist the temptation to travel into town, to stand in the vicinity of the house and observe the comings and goings. But she knows this is absolutely the last thing she must do. She has to endure the waiting however much it costs her emotionally. She tries to sleep but spends hours going over and over in her head the experiences she's had. Wants to touch herself as she remembers what they did for her but somehow can't bring herself to do it. A realisation of the pale simulacrum a self-induced orgasm will be compared to the heights she's glimpsed so recently. But what if they don't want to see her again? How will she bear that disappointment? She can't begin to picture that.

As it transpires, she only has a few days to suffer the pangs of not knowing. When she gets up on Sunday morning to make herself a coffee, she finds an envelope on the mat beneath her doormat. It's an envelope made from an expensive, cream-coloured parchment. Inside on matching paper a simple message. 'Wednesday 8pm. As before.' There's no signature. Nothing else. But she doesn't need anything else. The short message is all she needs to put her into a state of elation. The world is suddenly a beautiful place again. Now she thinks *All I have to do is get through the next four days.* Somehow she does.

Wednesday arrives and Catherine's levels of anticipation are sky-high. She readies herself with care.

She's bought herself several pieces of new clothing. Not much different to what she's worn on previous Wednesdays. But new. Bought for herself but with the Master very much in mind. She dresses herself in them now. A silky skirt, slightly longer than her old one but so light, the slightest movement creates a swishing against her legs she finds incredibly sexual and trusts they will too. A deep grey bodice in the finest cotton with mid-length sleeves finished with drawstring ties. When she tries it on in the shop, her breathing becomes ragged, thinking about being tied up. New lingerie. Black and expensive. A waste perhaps if the panties are to be cut from her body as happened last time but the feel of the sheer material against her breasts, her tummy and her pubis is worth the price she pays. New eight denier hold-up stockings. The only thing she's wearing that's nor brand new, apart from a little dab of aromatic perfume between her breasts, is her boots. She sits to put them on.

When she rises to her feet the added height the boots give her adds to how good she feels about herself. She crosses to the long mirror behind her bedroom door and checks her appearance. *Pretty good for a plain girl* she thinks. But she's not plain at all and she knows it. She practices smiling at her reflection. At the tall young woman in the mirror with the shoulder-length brunette hair. Late twenties but with her looks and clear complexion, she knows she can pass for much younger. She's pleased with the hang and fit of her new clothes. With the way they cling to and reveal her body. Above all with how they complement and fuel her rising excitement.

She can't keep still now but it's way too early. She takes herself into her lounge to wait for the taxi she's ordered. Forces herself to sit demurely in one of her armchairs. Crosses her legs but the rasp of her stockings against each other brings into mind the thought of a stranger's hands massaging her legs, enjoying the way the nylon clings to her smooth calves. Whatever she might do by way of displacement activity; making herself a cup of tea, turning on the television, picking up a book; will be useless and she knows it. And so she sits and watches the clock on the mantelpiece, falling into such a reverie of anticipation that the ringing doorbell comes as a complete surprise to her until she realises it must be her taxi-driver. At last.

Catherine Rei stands, smooths herself down and opens the door.

6 ~ SCHOOLING

Among the things Catherine Rei appreciates most in her life are her routines. It's not that she can't appreciate change but she likes a degree of security. And so walking into the big house, being greeted by and giving her jacket to the butler and being ushered into the now familiar ante-chamber are all welcome precursors to whatever is likely to be happening to her body next. She anticipates being blindfolded, being led helplessly to wherever she needs to be and placed as they desire. The thought of ceding control to that pattern is already making her wet. Her labia inside the expensive knickers are moist. If she was to be fingered now…well they would slide easily across and into a well-lubricated channel.

She sits on the burgundy velvet upholstery in anticipation of what is to come. Or more precisely what is to make her come.

And then, to her instant disappointment, the expected routine is broken.

The door opens to admit two men dressed identically. Completely in black, she's never seen them before. Silky black shirts, black jeans and thick rubber-soled black canvas trainers. Neither of them the tall man with the comforting presence and gentle hands she realises suddenly she's desperate to have at her side. These men have neither his height, his courteous manners nor his reassuringly slow approach.

"Stand up."

Dismayed, she obeys swiftly. Can't quite control a nervous fluttering in her thighs.

More abrupt commands. "Get undressed. Leave your stockings on. Do it!"

Understandably perhaps, she feels she wants to cry. Doesn't but only by making a heroic effort to concentrate on the mechanical tasks of disrobing. She stands awkwardly, stork-like, on one leg to remove a boot. Switches legs to take off the other one. Unbuttons her top. Undoes the lace ties on each sleeve so she can get it off without tearing the stitching.

"Get a move on!" A coarse tone. Estuarial English. And the lascivious way they're looking at her is frightening.

Catherine blanks out the reality of what's happening. Pictures herself undressing in the safety of her own home. Places the blouse carefully down on the settee. Refuses to just drop it. She reaches behind her back to unfasten her new bra. Takes that off and puts it down on top of the blouse. As she bends her breasts swing out from her torso inviting touch. She half expects to be grabbed and manhandled. It doesn't happen.

Her skirt follows next. A button to be unhooked and a hidden side zipper to be undone before she can step out of it. She lays it on the pile. She has no real hope that she'll be allowed to keep her panties on but she looks across to check the implacability of their expressions before she slides them off and lays them down with the rest of her clothes.

The shorter of the two men holds out a piece of fabric she realises he's had in his hand ever since coming into the room. Catherine takes it. Shakes it out. Sees what it is. And puts on the sheer black robe with the single button at her throat to hold the garment together. It conceals nothing. Indeed it enhances and frames her body. Will reveal everything she has and is as she moves in it.

The other man has something in his hands too. Lays down what he's been carrying on the floor in front of her. For her to step into. A pair of low-heeled mules. Soft black leather uppers. The shoes fit her feet perfectly. She asks herself the obvious question. *How did they know my size?* Says nothing aloud although the silence is overwhelmingly hard to bear.

"Come".

Catherine is not so disconcerted that she can fail to spot that a mistake has been made. They've forgotten to blindfold her. She wonders if she should say something but it's not her error and she'll be bound to be in the wrong if she speaks out. She stays silent. Following the shorter man out into the hall, his companion behind her.

Three paces across the hall. To another door. The man ahead of her knocks twice on it. And after a second or two gets the expected response. "Come in." He opens the door. Stands aside to let Catherine enter. Doesn't come in with her. Closes the door behind her.

The room is a large square space, sparsely furnished. In the centre a low platform with a high-backed wooden chair placed upon it. Directly in front of the dais is a long table and sitting behind it six people. Catherine is positive this must be the room she sat in on her first visit to the house. Without needing any instruction to do so, she walks across the room. No, she doesn't just walk. With a rising confidence she sashays across the floor, fully aware of the impression she must be making as her long legs part the sheer black robe and her breasts, the perfectly shaped breasts with the tiny roseate nipples of which she has every reason to be inordinately proud, are displayed and covered, displayed and re-covered for them. For the members of the Forum. For their enjoyment. And as it seems for her own.

Without waiting for any instruction, Catherine negotiates the step up and settles onto her chair. The wooden seat is hard, unpadded under her bottom. She wiggles a little re-discovering its shape and how it can best accommodate her. Only then does she look up. And realise that the lack of a blindfold for her was wholly intentional.

The faces of every one of the six men and women sitting behind the table facing Catherine are covered. Instead of human faces she sees a line of cruelly styled Venetian masks. Black, silver or harlequin. Some with arrogantly protruding false noses. One in particular shaped like an up-risen phallus. Another feathered, giving the wearer the look of some large exotic bird of prey. The effect is like a dousing of cold water for Catherine. All her confidence is gone in a flash. The room suddenly seeming too cold for the little she has on. She shivers. Her skin goose-bumps. But perversely her nipples are erect again. She tries hard to control her fear and is thankful to be sitting down, able to grip the arms of the wooden chair and hide the slight quivering which would otherwise be apparent in her hands.

Someone speaks. A familiar voice. With that slight accent. "Welcome back, Catherine Rei." And as suddenly as the fear came, it's gone and a calmness settles over her.

He continues. "Tonight is inquisitorial. Part of getting to know who you really are. Finding out what makes you tick. So that the Forum can meet your deepest needs. And judge to what degree you will satisfy ours. Does that make sense to you, Catherine?"

Dry-mouthed, she clears her throat. "It does."

A different voice asks the next question of her. Although a seated position disguises his height and a be-jewelled mask his features, Catherine is fairly sure it's the tall man asking her "Did you enjoy what was done for you; with you; to you; last week?"

"Yes." Catherine can't think of anything to add to her answer.

The questioner prompts her. "What in particular did you find to enjoy?"

She decides to be frank. The only possible approach. "You made me come. I've never come like that before."

"Ah. Do you mean so intensely or do you mean in that fashion?"

"I mean both."

"Indeed. Have you ever been in bondage before?"

"Tied up? No I haven't"

The Master intervenes. "You weren't tied up, child. You were strapped to a bed. There is a difference as I promise you will discover."

The questioner smoothly continues his line of enquiry. "How did being helpless make you feel?"

Catherine considers the question carefully. There is no simple answer she can give. "It's complicated. I suppose I was nervous. But you made me feel safe."

"But not excited?"

"Not...No. But I did when the people came and touched me."

"I see. Was there something in particular that excited you then?"

"It was...That I couldn't touch them back. Touch you. I had to lie there. And let you do whatever you wanted to do. And...It was very exciting for me."

"Did you ever think about how being held down and petted and kissed would feel? Is it something you've fantasised about?"

"Well...no."

"There's something there isn't there? Something you're not saying. What is it? Don't be afraid. We will not judge you harshly. Whatever you tell us."

"When I was at school..."

"Yes. And...?"

Catherine gulps. Starts to reply. Can't get the words out."

One of the women intervenes. "Would you like a glass of water? Max...?"

"No names here." The Master cutting across her. A hint of real anger. "You know better than that."

But her tall man is already bringing a full glass across to her. And now she knows his name.

"When you're ready."

"It was a fairly small grammar school. A mixed sixth form. And I was a prefect."

"How old were you?"

"Seventeen I think then. It was before I turned eighteen. Anyway we had a common room. The teachers never came there. It was ours." She stops.

"And what happened?"

"Well..umm. There was a boy called Micky. He was really cocky. But funny. And quite good looking. And one morning there was just him and me in the common room and...He was trying it on with me. We had all this old furniture. Like settees and a microwave and some desks. We were on the settee messing about. And I didn't mind him doing...He was touching my breast through my shirt and trying to kiss me. And I was kissing him back a bit. And the door opened and these three other prefects came in. And Micky didn't just stop. He said out loud *Katie's hot today. Come and feel.* I could have stopped them then. But something inside me didn't want it to stop. There wasn't room on the settee for all of them so they picked me up bodily and put me down on the snooker table. And they were holding me down and their hands were everywhere. Inside my blazer and shirt. And they got my bra pulled down so they could grab my bare tits." She smiles as she says it. Acknowledging to herself how appropriate the cruder language she's falling into is. "And then one of them got his hand up my skirt and into my knickers. It wasn't Mickey. It was one of the others. Not one of the good-looking ones. He was skinny and wore glasses. But he was like desperate to touch me. And they're holding me down and fondling my breasts and this creep's trying to frig me. And the strangest thing...The minute his fingers got into me, I started to come. I didn't think I wanted to. But...I just did. I don't know why."

"And that was a one-off experience?"

Catherine takes a sip of water. "No. To be honest it wasn't. I sort of engineered it to happen again a couple more times. But whatever they were doing to me, I only came when the creepy kid touched my pussy."

Silence falls in the room. Catherine slumps back in the chair relieved to have a momentary relief from the questions. The rest isn't a long one.

The Master breaks the silence. "You've told us this story. How do you feel now?"

"I've always been a bit shocked that I let it happen."

"I didn't mean that. Does telling us turn you on?"

And a real shock hits Catherine. She hasn't appreciated till now what relieving the past has done to her. Her pussy is soaking and she's sticking to the seat. "Oh my God. I'm sorry."

"There's no need to apologise. We wanted this. You realise there's much more we want to ask you about. But there's no more time now. Other business to transact I'm afraid. And somebody else waiting for us. But we can't leave you in this state. I suspect we can spare one of our number for now."

Catherine's tall man gets to his feet and comes round the table to her. She starts to stand up herself but he doesn't let her. "Put your arms round my neck." She does as she's told and he picks her up without much difficulty, one arm supporting her back and the other under her knees. Somebody holds the door open for them to pass and Max carries her up the stairs to a darkened side-room and lays her down carefully on the bed.

She doesn't mean to beg but when she says, "Don't leave me," it comes out as a plea.

"I have no intention of leaving you just yet." And he chuckles at the absurdity of the thought.

7 ~ MAX

Max walks over to close the door. Takes off his mask. Comes back to the bedside.

"Shove up a bit."

Catherine edges over to make room for him to lie down beside her. He pushes an arm around her shoulders and rolls her over onto him. Her left palm settles on his cheek, turning his head so she can put her mouth to his. His hand brushes aside her flimsy robe and cups her luscious breast. She sits up abruptly, a decision made she intends to implement. Pulls at him until he lets her pull off his shirt. Crouches to untie his shoes and remove his socks. He takes advantage of her position to firmly trace the contours of her arse, tempted to put her over his knee and spank her. But doesn't. That would be to impinge on the programme the Master's laid down for her.

He helps her by removing his trousers and pants. Lays down beside her again. Her thigh now rests on his naked leg and he leaves the next move to her. She starts on him. Confidently exploring his body. Her hands cupping his balls and stroking his hardening cock. There's no need for him to do anything except follow her lead. And she grasps his waist, encouraging him across and onto her. She's so open and wet that he slides straight in. Begins to move with her heels kicking the back of his thighs, urging him to move faster and deeper inside her. In the semi-darkness her head is flung back over the edge of the pillow and the expression on her face is as ecstatic as the little gasps she's making.

It doesn't take long for either of them to finish. He isn't sure she actually comes as he empties himself inside her but she cries out and hugs him tightly to her body. Won't let him go even as he tries to use his elbows and knees to keep his weight off her. Eventually she lets him slump sideways. Curls herself into him so his warmth seeps through her skin. And then she sleeps.

Sometime before daybreak she comes awake to find a coverlet over her. Panics that he might be gone. But an out-flung arm collides with his solid bulk. Satisfied she settles back into slumber. Quietly confident that she'll have him again before she leaves in the morning.

8 ~ UNCERTAINTY

Catherine spends the next seven days torn between hoping that the rules will change and she'll see Max and knowing that she won't until next Wednesday, the date on the card pushed into her handbag that morning after the last time. And then she won't really be seeing him. Won't have him to herself. She'll be blindfolded and at the mercy of them all. Or he'll be masked so she can't see what he's really thinking and feeling about her. Because those are the terms of her engagement with the Forum. Part of her could almost walk away from the solemn undertakings she's made. If only it would guarantee Max's continuing presence in her life. But her more rational self is certain of her need to see this journey through. That what she's experiencing and being taught about herself are invaluable to her future happiness. So she has no choice. No real choice but once again to be patient and see what next Wednesday will bring her.

At the due time she dresses on automatic pilot. Donning the black silk underwear, the blouse, skirt, stockings and boots which are to all intents and purposes now the uniform of her sexual enslavement. Her emotional captivity. Her excitement is muted. She's not entirely sure she even wants to go to the house again today. She could of course stay home and it would be over. But somehow she can't. She doesn't.

The taxi delivers her to her destination in around twenty minutes. Twenty minutes in which she does a lot of thinking. And the conclusion she reaches involves an honest appraisal of herself and a life in she thinks of herself as loving the security of regular routines but in which she's never really stuck to anything, giving up relationships at the merest hint of a problem, changing jobs whenever she felt like it and moving homes simply for the novelty. *If I don't see this through, I'll never finish anything*, she reasons. And indecision departing, she begins to feel the nervous stirrings of sexual excitement again and she knows it's going to be better than alright. Whatever comes with the night ahead.

9 ~ AT THE BOTTOM

The butler. The ante-chamber. The waiting. And after a while a smiling Max carrying the scarf which he turns deftly into a blindfold for her. Whispers in her ear as she crosses the hall leaning on his arm. "Are you alright?"

"Yes." Grateful to him for asking.

Catherine assumes her obligatory seat. And without being asked to do so, separates her knees so the Forum's members can see up her skirt.

"Good evening, Catherine. Is everything well with you?"

What is this? Why is everybody concerned about me now? "Yes. It is."

"Then we have more questions for you. Our colleague will handle you tonight." *A strange way to put it,* Catherine thinks. *A double entendre or just a clumsy form of speech?*

A woman's voice takes over. It's deliberately pitched low and husky. "Cast your mind back to the first night you came before us. You told us you'd never been tied up before. Is that correct?"

"It is."

"I want you do something for us know. Stand up and turn to face away from us". Catherine obeys on the instant and without question. "Good. Now please raise your skirt and take down your knickers."

A rush of blood to her face is matched by the knowledge that her labia are engorging too. She puts her hands at each side of the waistband and bends as her panties descend.

"Step out of them. Leave them on the floor. Now kneel up on the chair. Show us your bottom. Can you spread your cheeks for us please?" Her face is flaming but she's mercifully able to hide it from them, turned this way round.

"Perhaps a cushion."

Gentle hands slide something under her knees. A great relief. She couldn't have held this position long on the bare wood of the chair.

"Is that any better?"

"Yes, thank you...Mistress." The last word comes unbidden and without conscious thought. It seems right. Nobody comments.

"You have a very beautiful arse. It invites certain...attentions. Have you ever been punished?"

Catherine begins to panic. She doesn't understand the purport of the question. And then she remembers that she's allowed to seek clarification when necessary.

"I'm sorry. I don't follow..."

The tone of voice of the woman asking questions doesn't change a jot. She sounds calmly unhurriedly. And perfectly willing to explain. "Has anybody ever spanked or caned or whipped you?"

"No. Never."

"You know what I'm going to ask you next, don't you?"

"I think so."

"Does the thought of being punished like that excite you."

Catherine finds it hard to answer with any volume. Her voice is not much more than a whisper when she says "Yes."

The Master comes in with an instruction plainly aimed at her rather than for her. "Take her and prepare her." She's seized on the moment by a man to each side of her and carried backwards out of the room, still in a quasi-kneeling posture.

Everything seems to happen very swiftly. Traversing the hall, she's taken into another chamber she's not been in before. She's dumped ignominiously on the floor and half stripped. Her boots, stockings and skirt are taken off her. She's picked up by the waist and carried a few steps. "Bend over. Put your arms out. And lower your head." Her throat rests on a shaped piece of wood as do her wrists. "Stand still now." A block is drawn down across the back of her neck. The same block secures her wrists in place. She hears the click of a lock. And then she's standing on the balls of her feet and there's little latitude for further movement. The blindfold has shifted slightly and she has a narrow field of peripheral vision to her left but it doesn't help her much. The room is dimly lit and there's nothing before her except for drawn curtains.

Left to stand there awkwardly, only now is she given the opportunity to ponder what's going to happen next. And for fear to begin to dry up the leaking wetness between her legs.

She has no idea of time. How long she's left unattended. It may be only minutes in fact but it feels far too long. When she hears the door re-open she's relieved that whatever is coming next will be starting. But it's only one of the attendants who moves across in front of her to open the curtains a fraction, letting more light into the room. But he doesn't leave immediately. She feels his hand alight on her waist, gripping her, holding her still while with his other hand settles on her bottom. Cupping and squeezing and stroking it. Next he slides a thin piece of wood beneath her feet, making it easier for her to stand comfortably but he uses the extra play it gives to move her legs apart.

Wide apart. She hears him doing something else behind her but can't tell what it is until a generous dollop of some cool, gelatinous substance is dripped onto her lower back. Just above her bottom. Then his fingers get to work on her.

First he shifts the lubricant around and as her body warms it up, spreads it down between her legs, thickly coating the seam of her pussy and into the cleft of her arse. He works it in between the protruding leaves of her outer labia and up across her increasingly sensitised clitoris. Greases her perineum with it, the tender skin between her pussy and her softly puckered little notch. And finally with his thumb he gently massages it around and onto her arse-hole itself. It feels as though he leaves a disproportionate amount of the gel there.

Her senses are acutely attuned as she stands captive in the stocks. She hears a rustle of paper and interprets it as him wiping his hands. Then silence. He hasn't left the room as far as she can tell. She would definitely have heard the door latch. Is he standing there contemplating her half-naked body? She knows that's what he must be doing and his unseen admiration of her nether parts fires something in her. His gaze feels like something real on her skin. She can't rub her thighs together without shifting position and she's sure that's not going to be allowed her. But she wants some form of touch. Is beginning to want it desperately. And she sighs with pleasure as his hand returns, the hairs on his wrist tickling her as he moves it through her legs and a slow and very deliberate stroking of her pussy begins.

Catherine finds herself lost in the delightful sensations he induces. His lubricated fingers sliding easily around on her. More readily still as her own juices flow. She's dimly aware in the haze of her growing excitement that whilst his fingers are working her labia, his thumb is tracing tiny circles around her anal sphincter. If it hurt; if he was using any real pressure, she would want to protest. But it doesn't hurt. He's just touching her firmly but gently and soon in the rising heat of the other sensations, she forgets his thumb is there at all.

A finger dares to steal just inside the lips of her overheated vagina. To moving rhythmically. Stretching her. And then exploring deeper inside her. There's no resistance. Just a flood of viscous moisture to tell him how much he's exciting her. The second finger joins the first. And now there's alternate pressure and release inside her pussy. She groans. Wants to tell him not to stop but dare not break the silence. Let's out little mews to try to communicate the same message without words. She tenses, her body rising onto her toes. And relaxes sinking back down on the piece of wood under her feet. She's so very close to coming. And he stops.

She can't help it. The groan of sheer frustration is not of her conscious volition. She wants his fingers moving again. But he holds them still inside her. She tries to grip them using the muscles of her pelvic floor. But what begins to move isn't his fingers. It's his thumb. Lost in the sensations he's made her experience, she's been completely unaware of her bottom opening up under the infinitely steady and slow pressure he's brought to bear. And his thumb, now buried completely inside her rear passage, is the only thing moving inside her as he begins its steady removal in the face of the resistance that her belated realisation has caused.

And he speaks now for the first time. "Good girl," is all he says. And those two words make her flush with delight. As though his approval means everything in the world at this moment in time.

As he leaves the room, he slaps her bottom. Once only. Finely judged. And not hard. But it has a powerful effect. It causes a violent shudder in her and she almost comes then and there. But she isn't quite there yet. And isn't meant to be.

10 ~ CANING

Catherine is alone for no more than minutes. The door opens and it's obvious to her that several people are now in the small room with her. Without thinking about it, she abandons the more comfortable position she's adopted and spreads her legs apart. A hand alights on her up-tilted bottom. Rubs it briskly. Somebody else moves across in front of her. With her limited vision all she can tell is that it's a man. Until without warning the scarf is pulled off her face. Even the limited light means a few seconds for her eyes to adjust before she can focus on the person in front of her. She only knows it isn't Max. Not tall enough. He's wearing only black. As they all do. More significantly he's wearing a contoured mask over the upper half of his features so she's none the wiser for no longer being blindfolded. Except that his chin is dimpled in the centre. *Like that old film star* she thinks. And his mouth is thin-lipped giving an impression of cruelty. When he starts to speak her impression of him is dispelled by the softness of his voice and then by what he leans in close to whisper in her ear. "This will hurt. But very briefly. Count each stroke. There will six and then it'll be all over. Do you understand?"

She says "Yes" but is thrown completely because the next sensation is the diametrical opposite of pain. Fingers touch and caress the entire area around her vulva and she relaxes as the pleasure begins to take her away. They must have sought that response because it's only when the hand is lifted away that the promised pain arrives. A brisk swishing sound and a slashing instant of agony across both cheeks. She screams. She can't help herself.

The masked man before her says something. "Ssshhh." And strokes her hair. "Remember to count. One."

Dully she realises he means she must respond. "One". And the hand is back between her legs. Stroking her.

And so it goes. The sound of the cane travelling through the air. The line scored across her arse. The shriek she tries so hard not to make. Trying to remember to count. "Two." The fingers back on her pussy, rubbing and gently pulling. Swish. "Three." "Four." "Five." "Six." And it's done.

Now the fingers are given free rein to drive her rising excitement, pushing deep inside her. Twisting and separating. She grunts. Demanding more. As they're driven in and out of her more forcefully. And she comes. In relief screaming almost as loudly as under the strokes of the cane.

Again the same simple compliment as before. "Good, girl." And the weight of the block is lifted off her neck and her upper body released. She totters slightly as she straightens and someone catches her by the waist. Supports her until she can manage to stand on her own. It's a woman's arm around and her shoulder and she smiles her gratitude. Towards the face clad in feathered simulation of an owl.

11 ~ IN RECOVERY

Catherine is too exhausted not to sleep that night but sitting down at her desk the next day is going to pose very real problems. Before getting dressed she examines the damage in her full-length bedroom mirror. Craning her head around over her shoulder she can see her reddened and bruised bottom carries six very clear stripes. Four horizontally placed at precise intervals between coccyx and upper thigh and two cuts angled to bisect the others. It's the last two which hurt the most.

The only thing she can find to rub carefully onto her wounds is the remaining half a bottle of after-sun cream left over from last summer. It will have to do until she can get something better from the chemists.

She finds the oldest and softest cotton underwear to put on under her work suit. And is grateful that the crowded tube means she won't look out of place by standing in a carriage with empty seats.

The day in the office is a nightmare though. In her own cubicle she can readily work after a fashion without using her chair but her boss sadistically calls a team meeting mid-morning which goes on and on and on. Were he not a happily married, dumpy, middle-aged man, she might think it possible for him to know of her stricken condition. But extreme conspiracy theory aside, she dismisses immediately the idea that he could be an associate of the Forum. It's just unfortunate that his desire to maunder on today about sales targets should coincide with the extreme discomfort her well-punished bottom is causing her.

It being a lovely sunny day, lunch can be taken in sandwich form on the street but her afternoon isn't much better than the morning apart from the fact that the meetings are shorter and in different locations within her company's office block so at least she can intermittently enjoy the relief of a short walk or a journey in the lifts before having to settle herself gingerly onto a seat once more. If it didn't hurt so much she'd worry that a colleague might notice her involuntary winces but nobody comments and the cock and bull story she's been rehearsing about falling over whilst hoovering is neither needed nor deployed.

The joy of being able to depart for home at half past five, with the imminent prospect of a hot and soothing soak, is indescribable. Walking into her home leads without delay to kicking off her shoes and shedding all her clothes. Even discarding the well-worn knickers is a major contribution to feeling better about life. And subsiding into her foaming bath borders on the heavenly. After topping it up with hot water a couple of times, Catherine feels sufficiently recovered to explore the damage. With care naturally. The flagrant effect of her caning seems slightly reduced so far as she can ascertain and touching the stripes brings back recollections of the pleasuring which accompanied their delivery. With certain inevitable consequences. Her hands stray to another part of her anatomy and she finds herself masturbating. Slowly at first but soon more desperately until she comes, sloshing copious amounts of water onto the bathroom floor.

She lies there a bit longer until she realises the bath's getting cooler. Pulls the plug out with the chain between her toes but instead of getting out, jams it back in a few moments later, adds more hot water and starts to touch herself again. Less directly and slower but leading in time to the same conclusion as before. An impressively easy climax, at the peak of which she can clearly picture in her mind's eye a man dressed entirely in black feeding his fingers into her expectant pussy. But in her reverie the man frigging her to orgasm is Max.

Again sleep comes readily and deeply. Fuelled by an oddly perverse pride in what she was able to withstand that night. But every day she wakes to find her bottom recovering a little more from its ordeal. In the mirror, the bruising is going down and the stripes of the cane are becoming less individually distinct. Above all else she notices how much easier it is becoming to sit down. *It's just as well* she thinks because the anticipated summons for a fourth Wednesday meeting of the Forum in a row has appeared on her doormat. And as each day passes and the memory of the pain of her caning becomes hazier, leaving only an enhanced memory of the strength of her orgasm at the end of it, she's coming to see that she could readily endure it all again. If she has to.

12 ~ VIRGINITY

Wednesday's here. Mid-evening to be precise. And Catherine's sitting once again on the wooden seat of the high-backed chair with the sculpted arms on which she rests her hands, ready to grip if nerves get the better of her. But in fact she feels increasingly comfortable here, blindfolded with the black silk scarf, her legs parted to reveal her stocking tops.

The Master wants to know about her reaction to being beaten.

"Well it hurt obviously. It hurt a lot."

"But afterwards you came. You came very hard didn't you?"

A simple admission to make. "Yes".

"So if I have you taken away and caned again, you wouldn't object?"

"I would rather you didn't. It's taken me all week to be able to sit down comfortably." A ripple of laughter greets that observation. "But I couldn't object. I want to carry on. I'll do whatever you tell me to do. Nothing that's happened changes that." The longest answer to a direct question Catherine Rei's given in this room.

"Alright." Somehow she can hear the smile in the Master's voice. "The good news then is that you won't be thrashed again. Not tonight. We don't seem to have got very far with cataloguing your sexual history for our records. Tell us this. When did you lose your virginity?"

Catherine's panic is immediate. And total. "Why do you need to know that?"

"It doesn't matter why. The deal is that we ask you questions and you answer them. And it would be a shame to send you home now. At this stage when you've made such progress so quickly."

Catherine thinks furiously. Tries to bargain. "If I tell you what you want to know, does it stay here in this room?"

"Why do you need to ask that?"

"Because it's somebody else's secret too. And I can't see them...hurt."

"Then you have to trust us." A very sharp edge apparent. "Answer the question."

The resulting silence continues until Catherine's resolve breaks. She clears her throat. "It's hard to talk about."

Evoking a more understanding response. "I know it is. But tell us anyway. Get it off your chest and you'll feel better. There are no secrets here within the Forum. We believe in truth and openness. And we already care about you Catherine. We promised that if you were open with us we would not hurt you. I remind you that this is a two-way street in which we each trust and give to each other. Now in what circumstances did you lose your virginity?"

Catherine knows she has to tell them but doesn't know where to start. Unless at the very beginning. "My mother died when I was little and I was brought up by my father and a succession of au-pairs and house-keepers. I suspect he slept with most of them so I wasn't Daddy's darling little girl. Not really. He re-married when I was thirteen and he tried to pretend we would turn into a proper family; me, him, my step-mother and my new step-brother, Stephen. It didn't happen. The family thing. She tried to like me but I was very difficult. I did a lot to alienate her. The problem was Stephen. He was quiet and really nice. Always had his head in a book. He was almost two years older than me. And I liked him. But I kept provoking him too. I wanted his attention. And his company. And one day I got it..."

She pauses. "Could I have some water, please."

"Yes. Get her some please."

Taking a sip eases her tightened throat and allows her to carry on. "I went into his bedroom one day. It was always me who went to him. Never the other way round. And he was there, lying on the bed reading. And I sat down next to him. And he wouldn't put the book down. So I started to tickle him. And he grabbed my hands to stop me..."

"And he tried to kiss you?"

"No. Not that. He was quite strong and he took both my wrists in one hand and got his leg between my knees and he put his hand under my t-shirt. I didn't really have breasts then although they were coming. And he said I was lovely. And I had to stop teasing him. And I said that wasn't going to happen. And he...ran his hand right down my body. He undid the waist button on my jeans. It was winter and I was cold. I'd got tights on under my jeans. And he said he liked how it made my skin feel. Touching me through the nylon. And he put his hands down inside my knickers. And I wasn't struggling anymore. He'd let go of my hands. And it felt...I remember felt really funny and weird. But very excited until eventually I made him stop."

"And...?"

Another sip of water. "Two days later, I'm back on his bed again, letting him touch me. It happened a lot after that. He got so good at it. He'd diddle my clitoris between two fingers and he found it so easy to make me come. He let me undo his jeans. He wouldn't let me see his cock for quite a long time. But he let me hold it. I loved how it got so hard so quickly in my hand. And the shape and feel of his balls. I was completely hooked. A day when we weren't touching was a wasted day in my book. Of course the school holidays and weekends were when it was easiest. And we had a few close shaves when one or other of our parents walked in on us but we never put music on or anything so we could strain our ears to hear if someone was coming up the stairs so we'd button up our jeans and be innocently sitting there talking..."

"How long did this go on?"

"I don't know exactly. Eighteen months or so. Well after I turned fifteen anyway. What was strange was how easy we were with each other. We could tell each other anything. He loved my bottom and how he said it looked and felt in my tights. He got me to wear my tights under long skirts without any knickers on. He said letting my skirt fall down would be quicker than doing up my jeans if someone was coming. And that having the tights on would be less suspicious than bare legs. But really I knew it was because he liked to have my bottom in his hands in the tights. And to get his fingers into my pussy inside them. And when he finally let me see it I loved how his cock looked. He had this puff of dark hair at the base of it but his cock itself was so smooth. Especially compared to his balls. they were big and wrinkly. He wanted me to suck his cock but I thought that was dirty and I wouldn't ever do it. Now I wish I had..."

They're so caught up in her story, you could hear a pin drop when Catherine pauses. No-one interrupts and she starts again. "I'm not sure if I had a proper hymen. Early on he could get a finger right inside me and it didn't hurt at all. And soon he was pushing two or three into me. He was very slow and gentle but I made him do it faster. And then he started to let me make him spurt in my hand. And of course we were always going to take it further. We both knew it was only a matter of time. So that's how I came to lose my virginity."

She doesn't want to talk about the rest of it but she has to now. So more water and tell them all of it.

"He never pushed me into it. I knew he'd got some condoms so it'd be safe. And he told me sometimes how much he'd like to fuck me. Only he didn't say that. I think he said screw me. But he didn't make any great deal of it. Which is probably why I did it in the end. I was as curious as he was and I trusted him. And I thought about waiting till I was sixteen and legal. But in the end I didn't want to wait any longer. I wanted to know what his lovely, beautiful cock would feel like moving inside me. I thought it would be like his fingers but even better. So we waited one Saturday evening until our parents went out to the pub. And we did it. We lay down side by side on his bed and we took all our clothes off. We'd never done that before. Not completely. And he went ape over my breasts. Kissing and holding them. And he said he would kiss my pussy too. But he was too excited. So I helped him get the condom on. And it was a bit awkward. He was trying to balance on his knees and one hand while he got his cock in the right place. But I helped him with that too. And then he was in me. He slid in just like that. And it was like a wonderfully strange thing. It wasn't actually as exciting as when he caressed my clit but it was... really comforting. loving. Because he just lay on me. This weight on my pelvis and the length of him inside me. Not moving. But I could feel every inch of him in me. And after a bit he started to move in me and he was shivering and I knew he wouldn't last much longer. And I wasn't coming but it didn't matter. It was as good a first time as I'd hoped it would be. And I wanted to feel him spurting. See if I could feel that through the condom. And I was already thinking about the next time. How with this barrier crossed...what we'd do next. How good we'd get at pleasing each other. Learning it over a long time. Just like it was with finding out about each other's bodies and how to touch each other. But that was the first and only time. He was nearly there...And..." Time to be really matter of fact now. "The door crashed open. We'd been ages and we were making a bit of noise and we didn't hear our parents come back. It was my Step-Mum. She hauled him off me. She was screaming at us. Calling me a tramp and a whore and a slut. And going on about her precious boy like it was all my fault when I'm fifteen and he's nearly seventeen. We were separated after that. Odd though it was him they sent away. To his aunt's and then to university. It was so bad at home, I gave it a few months and then left myself. I was sixteen by then and got a job. I never went back again."

"Have you seen any of them since? Stephen?"

"No. I know my father's dead now. But he took her side. Blamed me for breaking up his family as he put it. So I don't have a family anymore."

The Master's voice. Calming her but still posing questions. "Is that why you came to us? To the Forum? To find a new family?"

She would never have thought of it like that. "Perhaps."

"Catherine. You're braver than you know. And in truth I speak for all of us when I say that if you see out your initiation you have found a home with us. We want you to succeed. We want you. And I think you deserve a reward for your strength and honesty. We need to change our plans for the evening which requires a short discussion within the Forum. I'm going to have you escorted back into the ante-chamber where I want you to sit and rest for a few minutes. Keep your blindfold on and someone will be along to fetch you in due course. We won't be long."

"Thank you." Simple instructions to obey. So, she does.

13 ~ COMFORT AND KINDNESS

As Catherine's discovering for herself, removal of one sense intensifies others. Temporary deprivation of her sight increases the sensitivity of and her reliance upon her hearing in particular. The click of the door latch may be at the limits of audibility and the thick carpet may largely muffle footsteps but she's sure someone's come into the room and isn't surprised to find Max kneeling in front of her clasping both her hands between his. Even before he says a word, she knows it's him. From his personal scent and something about the quality of his touch on her skin.

"The Forum would have subjected you to another test tonight. But that's postponed for now. And before you ask I can't tell you what it should have been. The Master's view is that you need comfort and kindness. And for some reason...I've been unanimously appointed to be your guardian angel from here on in. I think everyone's noticed that it's a role I've already fallen into. And they think you'll respond better to me than anyone else."

Catherine says nothing. He'll see her smile and it'll tell him everything he needs to know.

Max helps her to her feet and guides her upstairs. Won't let her remove the blindfold. Takes her into a room with unusual acoustics and she realises it's tiled. But warm. And warm underfoot. Underfloor heating. "Stand right there a minute." He roots round in a cupboard and finds what he's looking for. A cord with which he can tie her wrists together and hitch her to a hook behind the door which he now takes the pre-caution of locking.

When water starts to run her strong suspicion that they're in a bathroom is confirmed.

Max is beside her again. "I want to undress you so I didn't think this out very well". As he undoes the cord. Unbuttons her blouse and discards it. Her bra follows. And he reties her wrists and pulls them back up onto the hook. The position raises her breasts too. "This'll be a bit cold at first." He's right about that. She flinches as he soothes a lotion first into the strap marks across her back and over her shoulders and then onto the temptation of her breasts. The massage is far too prolonged and intimate to be regarded as merely psychologically relaxing. To be anything other than blatantly sexual.

Now he unfastens and drops her skirt. Gets her to step out of it. Followed by her tiny and tight black panties. Leaving her in just her boots and stockings. A low whistle of appreciation tells Catherine exactly how much he likes that view. Not that he takes long to move on. Dropping to remove each boot in turn and then to carefully roll down each of her stockings. More lotion. This time rubbed gently in until largely absorbed by her legs.

Leaves her for a few seconds to turn off the bath water. Swishing and splashing noises. And it's ready. He doesn't untie her. Merely unhooks the cord, picks her up and carries her across the room, lowering her slowly into a deep tub of deliciously hot and foaming liquid. Gently positions her so she can lie back in the bath. Difficult otherwise for her to do without use of her hands.

Catherine sighs in satisfaction. She's never in her whole life been cosseted like this.
She starts to slip into reverie but Max has no intention of leaving things there. Making circles across her body with a well-soaped cotton exfoliating pad, he attends to her feet, her legs and, sitting her up momentarily, her back and shoulders. Reaching underneath he does the cheeks and cleft of her bottom before switching to something altogether softer to bathe and caress her breasts and stomach. If he needs further motivation, the murmurs and moans coming from

Catherine's mouth give it. He leaves his self-appointed task in the end only to run in more hot water, to strip off his own clothes and to join her in the massive bath. Settling in behind her, coiling his thighs around her hips, he draws her head back onto his shoulder. And his hands are free to roam. To tweak her hardening nipples and use the edges of his thumbs down into her groin.

She finds what he's doing to her highly arousing. And she's beginning to need much more and has to tell him so. "Max. Do the rules still apply tonight? Here with you I mean."

"They don't have to."

"So, I can say something to you?"

"Uh-huh."

"Will you untie my hands?"

"Do you need them to help you talk?"

"No. I need them because I want to touch you. And in particular I want to hold the hard thing that's poking me in the back."

"What's that then?"

"You know very well what that is."

"Let me have a quick search and see what comes up"

"It's already up. And you'd be having a lot more fun if you let me search for it."

More words would be nowhere near as eloquent a response as simply loosening the cord and slipping it off her wrists. Which she rubs briskly before reaching behind her to get to what she wants. Not, she finds, a sustainable position for very long. Much easier to pivot round to face him in the bath. Which also means she can see exactly what she's doing. And enjoy the appealing sight of the smooth helmet emerging from his retracting foreskin as she squeezes his cock.

"Come here you. If we're ditching the rules, there's one I definitely want to break". Pulling her slippery body up onto his so he can get his mouth onto hers. To enjoy a slowly deepening kiss, mashing their lips up together until it's more like they're eating each other, only coming up once in a while for air. And sitting on him, she gets her legs around his body and let's his perfectly positioned cock slip up between her labia, adjusting the angle of her pelvis until he just slides all the way up inside her.

"Oops".

"So, tell me I'm a clever girl".

"You're a wonderfully sexy, beautiful, clever girl".

"And I can do this". Internal muscles tightening and relaxing, milking him. She can feel him getting stiffer. Bigger. Trapped in her. Going nowhere. "And all thanks to yoga".

"Who's Yoga. I owe him or her a vote of thanks.

She cuffs him playfully round the head. Begins to move. Levering her body up and down on him. Letting his cock come most of the way out of her and then dropping herself all the way down again. A combination of rise and plummeting fall. Like a roller-coaster. Heading for the inevitable destination at the end of the line. Where she'll make sure she finishes first. Bucking harder now to bring herself off. Holding herself in place with her arms around his neck. Beginning to flush and shake on him. Making noises. Not words. Thrusting her body at him as well as onto him. "Oh God." Coming now. Her chest sweating and her head feverish with excitement. Slowing slightly to keep herself coming and coming. And the thrill as she feels him climax without warning. His semen shooting up high inside her. Coating her cervix. At least how she pictures what's happening. The rippling sensations taking her stratospheric. "God! God! God!" Unplanned recognition of the divinity of the moment. Subsiding now into its afterglow. Clinging on to Max in total gratitude for the way he's made her feel. Not wanting to get off him. If she could only stay in this moment a few more hours or even just a little longer. But his cock is softening and shrinking and soon it'll pop out because however much she tries; she won't be physically able to keep it inside her any longer.

14 ~ THE LINGERIE DRAWER

Catherine spends the night in a strange bed in Max's arms. She may not sleep much but feels marvellously alive in the morning. What she wants now is to take him out to breakfast somewhere with her. Not to have to let him go.

"I am sorry but we can't. You earned a suspension of the rules last night. But it doesn't apply today. And I'm bound by the rules too. You will be back here soon. The summons will come. And when it does I'll be here too. So be strong. Enjoy whatever happens next. And if it helps you when you're behind your blindfold know this much. Behind my mask, I'll be in your corner. Rooting for you. And thinking you quite the bravest and the most adore-able woman I could ever hope to meet. So till then. Okay?"

He kisses her. And shoos her out of the house. Tells her to go home and get ready for work. She's already late.

The summons he predicted is delivered the following day. It's there when she gets home from work and it wrecks any plans she might have had for the weekend. Because it sets her a new challenge. A hugely enjoyable one for a woman who loves clothes and shopping for them but one which promotes anxiety because she can't decide what could constitute rising successfully to it.

The card in the beautifully expensive envelope gives her the usual day and time in the following week to attend the Forum. But for the first time it does the opposite of specifying what she must wear. The summons simply includes the sentence *For clothing surprise us.*

Saturday and Sunday, and indeed every free moment of the first day of the new working week, are taken up with turning over ideas for stunningly sexy outfits, visiting photographic sites online to view the work of other costumiers, researching suppliers on the internet and doing the tiring legwork around the shops and arcades of Central London to find the things she thinks are worth trying.

By Monday night she's despairing of finding the right solution. She's tired and goes to bed hoping that something of her newly expanded wardrobe will do. After all she has the makings of at least five different approaches to her problem, one sweetly demure but demanding ravishment, one stunning in the way it will frame her legs in high heeled shoes, one imitative of the Classical Greek traditional in which she'll walk in baring her breasts, if she has the nerve, one redolent of a mid-twentieth century vamp and a last one which she knows will press every sexual button for the male members of the Forum but which she fears will have a counter-productive effect on the women.

In the process of assembling the outfits, she has dramatically expanded the amount of good lingerie she owns and when it's all unpacked, it may demand a second complete drawer in her bedroom. In this department she's spent a lot of money but has particularly enjoyed herself and feels she's bought wisely. Her favourite acquisitions are a balconette bra which shapes her breasts and presents her nipples naked to the world, a plain but beautiful black satin basque, an ivory lace set of panties, bra and suspenders, sets of expensive stockings, split equally between traditional and hold-ups and a couple of pairs of exquisite sheer-to-the-waist tights, which she's thinking the Master might approve of if worn without panties. Just thinking about sitting in front of the Forum with her legs spread and her pussy on show behind the smoky-coloured mesh gives rise to a lurching excitement and a rush of moisture down her sensitive seam. The problem remains though that she still doesn't know, from all her disparate ideas and purchases, how to present herself for the next meeting. Giving up, she goes to bed.

15 ~ VISION IN WHITE

They say sleeping on an issue can provide intuitive solutions because your mind works on while your body's unconscious. On this occasion that's certainly true and Catherine wakes to a eureka moment. It will mean a trip out at lunchtime to hunt something down but somehow she's confident her new idea will please.

At home with new bags to open, labels to cut off and a completely different affect to assemble. Starting with a quick bath and careful application of minimally subtle and effective make-up.

Dressed, she covers everything with a light raincoat. Picturing their surprise when she strips it off in front of them to reveal her chosen attire. Her excitement and apprehension somehow different, stronger than in previous weeks. Adding colour and tension to the taxi ride. Which not only lasts into the ante-chamber but grows incrementally as she waits to be called. It subsides only once she's sitting blindfolded in front of the members of the Forum. Still wearing her raincoat.

The protocol is clear. Sit and wait for instructions. Until the Master speaks.

"I take it the coat and shoes are not the sum of your chosen outfit." She's wearing plain white high heels.

"No, Sir."

"Then take them off."

She presumes he means the raincoat rather than the shoes. Stands to unbutton it and shuck it off. Lets it drop onto the floor around her feet. Her outfit is a very simple but effective negative of what she's been required to wear for past sessions. It throws the black scarf around her eyes into stark relief because her silk blouse and soft skirt are white. Her stockings are white. So are her high heels. When she sits down and opens her legs, they'll see her under things too are plain white. The only complicated thing to achieve about the way she looks is the plaiting of her hair. A friend from work helped her with that.

Nothing is said but she can feel the smiles of approval in the room. Kicks her raincoat away and sits to reveal the white lace of her stocking tops and the cotton panties covering her mound.

Without any comment or compliment on her appearance, the Master launches into the session with a new line of enquiry. "Tell us how much sex you've had. What's the highest number of times you've been fucked in one day?" His accent softens the crudity of the language. Renders the question less toxic.

"I had a boyfriend once who liked to just stay in bed with me..."

A murmured comment stops her in her tracks for a second. She thinks somebody muttered 'Who wouldn't' but can't be sure. It was a woman anyway.

"Please." Not aimed at her. An authoritative intervention. "Do carry on."

She does as she's told. "We would do it five or six times. Not that long each time. By the end my thighs would just cramp up and I could hardly walk."

"And what was the best sex you ever had? Was it with him?"

"No. Not really. The best was being so relaxed...with Stephen. Although we only...well I told you about what happened when we slept together. And then here with M..." Bites her tongue. "With the tall man you gave me to."

"Tell us about that experience. What did he do with you?"

The question is unexpected and disrupts her composure. Part of her doesn't want to talk about what Max did for her and how he made her feel. It's too new. She's not yet assimilated it. Worked out for herself what it means to her. And now she's being asked to do that with an audience. And in front of Max himself. She desperately doesn't want to do anything which would betray Max with his friends. Or upset him. But telling anything other than the truth isn't an option. She decides she has to be straight with them but underplay the significance of things if she can.

"I've had two nights with him...the tall man. And he's lovely. He looked after me. After you'd made me tell you stuff I didn't really think I'd be able to talk about, he calmed me down. He put me in the bath and got me totally relaxed. And when I went to bed with him, he was...I can't think of another way to put it. He was completely there. Into me. Absolutely focused on my needs. And it didn't ever feel like he was just screwing me. Most men I've known have been really selfish over sex. He wasn't at all. It felt like we were sharing something which made both of us happy. And... he made me come too and that's not always the case. In my experience."

"But when you described what happened to you at school with Mickey and the others, you seemed to be saying that an experience in which you were selfishly objectified also turned you on. Am I right in that?"

"I suppose so." She seems a little troubled by that deduction. Tries to explain it away. "They didn't know...didn't really care how I was feeling but it's still...What they did physically to me, my body responded to because it took my mind somewhere else. I can't find a better way to put it."

"And it was the same when you were tied to the bed?"

A shiver. "Oh yes."

"Being helpless? Forced to respond?"

"All those hands on me. It was...overwhelming."

"Then it's time for some practical reinforcement. The forum will adjourn now while Catherine's prepared for us."

A tiny hand-bell is tinkled. And that's a new departure. She's never heard that used before. Even in extremis, she'd have noticed. The door swings open and a double set of footsteps come straight for her. A hand under each elbow raises her to her feet and steer her out. And guide her upstairs.

She's not allowed to undress herself. It's obviously seen as a perk of the task for them to be able to fondle each part of her body as the removal of her clothes reveals it. One of them goes so far as to fleetingly suckle her right nipple as her bra drops away. Only her stockings are left in place as she's tied down. But it's different this time. She's not spread in place like a starfish. Her wrists are tied above her head but with some slack in the cord and her legs are left free. The blindfold stays in place however.

"She looks gorgeous, doesn't she? I'd like to see what she tastes like."

"But you can't, you mucky devil."

"Why not?"

"Because we weren't told we could. That's why not."

"Who's to know?"

"Don't."

The insistent one isn't going to be swayed. Catherine feels hands on her thighs. Parting them. And hot breath on her pussy. A head nuzzling in now and a mouth parting her labia. A cross between a kiss and a suck. A tongue running the length of her seam from her perineum to her clitoris. Tickling and then suddenly gone.

"Very sweet."

The door slams behind them and Catherine settles to the inevitability of waiting.

16 ~ EXTREMES

There is no wait to be endured. The door has hardly ceased quivering before it's flung open again and the room fills with people. Catherine has no way to know how many but assumes it's all six members of the Forum. And there is no interval afforded for contemplation of the inevitable. Hands are all over her naked body and somebody settles between her legs. Briefly fingers explore her slit but she's already wet enough and without pause something long and hard, indisputably male, begins to push inside her. She reaction is a completely natural response. To raise her knees. Her stockinged thighs grip the unknown man's waist and squeeze. He is a stranger too. His body not as lean as Max's. But she joyfully embraces penetration anyway. It's what she needs without knowing it beforehand. The cock thrusting into her. Deeper. Harder. Speeding up again. Spilling. But she can't feel his spurtings, except as twitchings of his cock. So he's using a condom. She doesn't care one way or the other now. She just wants to come herself.

The first stranger levers himself up and off her body. She feels opened, gaping. Needy. Until the next cock is inside her. A different shape. Bending upwards. Sporadically scraping her G-spot as he pushes into her. Raising her excitement to fever pitch. And her climax takes her by surprise. Shaking her whole body with its intensity. And then he's out and a third cock is pushing inside her. It could be Max and she's surprised at herself that she's not sure anymore if it is or not. Finds herself grunting. A guttural reaction as her re-arousal is driven to new heights. A sudden burst of light as the scarf is torn off and she screams at the cruelly leering face posed over her. Realises immediately, heart racing, that the stranger's wearing one of the Venetian costume masks. She looks down at the female hand playing with her breast. Senses the other accelerating movements on the bed. Turns her head and it's Max. But wearing another mask. But it has to be Max, lying alongside her fucking another naked woman. A slim body with surprisingly large breasts. No time for jealousy. She's coming again herself. Her vagina throbbing in ecstasy. Nearly blacking out. Exhaustion taking her. Wanting to curl up but the cock won't let her. Hasn't finished with her yet. Slowing down and thrusting in a deliberate rhythm of its own. Building its master's climax. And somehow she forms the belief that it is the Master who's going at her now. Pressing against her clitoris. Starting her moving again. When it's too much. When she's had enough. Is too weary to come again. But her treacherous body doesn't know that and is responding. Climbing up the ladder towards heaven. And he drives her into finishing simultaneously with him.

She sees him strip the full condom off his cock and toss it aside. Sees him tap Max with his fingertips. If it is Max. On his buttock. To get his attention. And Max rolls off the woman he's screwing. Cedes his place to the Master. Tears off his own condom. Now she's sure it's Max. Recognises the shape of his naked up-risen cock. And the feel of it as he plunges back into her. And if she thought herself too sore, too tired, too replete to come yet again, she's wrong, her pussy rippling beautifully as Max's semen sluices into her. She's aware of him crouching over her still. Of his weight on her body. Of his cock still inside her.

But she's asleep.

17 ~ PARANOIA

Catherine stretches luxuriously. Until she comes awake properly, but in a panic, remembering with startling clarity just what she did or what was done to her the night before. Aware of how sore her body is and wondering what he'll think of her now. Because Max's good opinion is, she realises, extremely important to her. It's still early but sunlight's creeping in through a gap in the curtains. And with relief she registers the arm lying across her belly, raising the covers to verify what she already knows in her heart. That it belongs to Max.

She prods him lightly. Gets no response. Reaches down and squeezes his cock. Which gets a reaction. His hand seizes her wrist, brings it up to his face and kisses her fingers.

"Don't think you're getting anything else this morning. I'm knackered." Max echoing her thoughts exactly. "How about a shower?"

"Sounds like a plan. I've got a bag somewhere. With a change of clothes and some make up in it."

"You came prepared this time."

"Certainly did. Thought after the last time...Having to race home in dirty gear to change. And getting grief for being late to work..."

"Your clothes will be outside the door. I'll bet. Nero will've taken care of them."

"Nero's the butler?"

"Yes."

"Is he really called Nero?"

"Well he answers to it. Probably not his real name though, I guess. Come on. Let's get in that shower."

And showering with Max is exactly what she needs. Having him soaping her back, holding her with one arm around her hips and across her tummy. Insisting on doing the front herself. "Not having you starting anything."

He groans. Mock resignation. "I'm not capable."

"Not sure I believe that." She takes the washcloth from him. Completes her ablutions. Rinses and re-soaps it. "Turn round. Your turn." And cleans his back. Reaches between his legs to soap his equipment, which contrary to his protestations shows some sign of burgeoning life. And finally washes his bottom for him. Lingering thoroughly with thoughts she has no intention of sharing with him here and now. At last says "There you go."

"Very professional." And wiggles his eyebrows at her to make her laugh.

Dressing is a blessing and a curse. A curse because if she had a free choice she'd far rather have the day with Max than go to work. A blessing because it armours her body against any further attempted assault from his curious hands. And she's way too sore down there to want that.

Goodbyes she handles briskly. Because she has to. Picks up her tote-bag, kisses his cheek, noting the slightly hurt look she gets when that's all she does, and heads out. He catches her at the bedroom door and kisses her properly before letting her go. It pleases her greatly that he won't settle for a perfunctory farewell. "See you soon, then." She manages a calmness in her voice she doesn't feel inside.

"You bet you will."

And she's gone.

Work? Well work is work. Dull by comparison with the night before. Tarnished by aches all over. Something to get through. Finally able to go home. Plans for a de-frosted pizza and an early night. Empties her handbag on the kitchen table to find her address book. And a familiar, sealed, cream envelope comes out with the jumble of everything else. She picks it up thoughtfully knowing full well that it wasn't there when she brought her sandwich back to her office for lunch. Which means that it was put there by somebody at work. And she goes cold at the thought. Her life works largely by keeping things compartmentalised. And yet somebody in her office is aware of her new sexual existence. She begins to worry.

And the worry doesn't let up. She's lost her appetite and can't sleep either, reporting for work on Friday, jaded and more than a little paranoid. She gets through the day somehow but when sleep proves elusive for a second night running, she knows she has to do something constructive to identify where the danger to her might be. Although she tells herself that whoever put the note in her handbag has to be someone trusted by the Forum and it's unlikely that messing up her life would meet with any kind of approval. So if he or she are sensible, they won't threaten to expose her. Nevertheless she wants to know who it is, if she can possibly find out.

Trying to proceed logically she finds a pad and pen and starts a list. A flurry of thefts of purses a few months ago made Catherine, along with most everybody else in the office, much more careful about personal belongings. And when she's away from her cubicle her handbag is either with her or locked in her desk drawer. Which means the only people who could have had access to it were those in the conference room or in other meetings with her on Thursday afternoon. And whoever it was must have been sitting next to her because she's positive she didn't leave it unattended anywhere.

The list is pretty short. Starts with the two colleagues flanking her at the conference table. She thinks about it and crosses out Jim from finance. She had the bag on the floor to her left. Jim would've had to reach across her to get to it. Then she attended a case review in Adam's cubicle. Her handbag was slung on the back of her chair so anybody could have slipped something into it. Three more potential suspects. And Koss and John both popped in to see her later in the afternoon. That's it then. One of six. Two of them very unlikely she feels. One approaching retirement. Just not the sort at all. Another a female trainee. The other end of the spectrum; too young. So three male; Adam John and Mitch; one female; Koss, short for Costanzia. A manageable list of possibilities. Except that a horrible thought occurs to her. Supposing it's not any of them but somebody else with access to master keys for the desks. Or the talent and tools to pick the lock. And the bottle to do it when someone could walk in at any moment. No. That's paranoia taken far too far. It's one of the four people on her list. It has to be.

18 ~ OVER THE KNEE

Catherine tries her hardest to put aside her suspicions of her colleagues. She can't let that spoil her anticipation of the coming Wednesday. Her mid-week high. To be faced nervously and with climbing adrenalin levels. Wondering what else could top all that last happened to her in the big house. The only thing she does know is that it won't duplicate her experiences so far. The note summoning her gave her no clue what to expect. Nothing beyond the date and time.

The day and time may be the same as in previous weeks but the arrangements aren't. On arrival, Nero opens the door to the ante-chamber and announces her arrival to the room in the manner of a toast-master at a charity ball. "Ladies and gentlemen. Miss Catherine Rei." And to her surprise, the Forum members are there waiting for her, lounging in comfortable chairs or standing by the tall windows. Every one of them is dressed head to toe in black and wears their chosen mask. The chattering stops abruptly at her entrance and her surprise at finding them all there brings her to a halt in the doorway.

"Come in, Catherine." Of course it would be for the Master to break the silence. He takes a step or two towards her, takes her arm and positions her where he wants her to stand, on the rug, centrally placed between three settees and the fireplace. Where a coffee table might normally be.

"To your places." The Master doesn't wait for the others to obey but sits. Makes himself comfortable, one leg crossed over the other, a foot dangling in mid-air, bouncing impatiently. Some of his colleagues rush to be seated. Others seem to drift lazily across the room. But finally everyone is settled and looking expectantly at Catherine, still standing there. She hasn't a clue what she's supposed to do.

"Strip!" An irritable tone. As though she should have been psychic enough to foresee his wishes. Catherine, back in black herself, unbuttons her blouse and without any fuss removes it and then her bra, her boots, her skirt and her knickers. The Master hasn't told her to stop so, after a fractional hesitation, she rolls down and takes off her stockings as well. Internally she observes that the process has ceased to make her nervous. She's become both accustomed and comfortable to being naked in front of these fully dressed people. She stands still now, awaiting instruction. Or interrogation. Neither is forthcoming. The Master makes a lazy gesture. Sketching a wave of his hand in the air. And getting to his feet it's Max. It has to be Max. Nobody else here is that tall. But in a different mask to last time. One which mimics a white ceramic shell emblazoned with three stylised teardrops on the left cheek.

Max picks up one of the cushioned chairs and carries it forward. Puts it down beside her. She makes a small movement towards it, expecting to be told to sit down. The Master doesn't miss a thing. "Don't move." And it's Max who sits on the chair.

"Now, Catherine. Over my knee." Max taps his right thigh with the flat of his hand. Indicating how he wants her. This way round. She remembers then something else she's learned about him. He's right-handed. She bends awkwardly to lower herself into position. Her head, shoulders, arms and breasts free, her stomach and core weight on his lap and her legs in space, until her feet find purchase on the rug.

"The time is right to demonstrate the value of a little...discipline."

Max starts to explain what's happening. Presumably by pre-arrangement for her benefit, although he's addressing the others as though delivering a formal lecture on the art and techniques of spanking. "To avoid excessive discomfort it's important to warm the area first. You'll notice that I'll be using a straightforward rubbing action and then a picking motion taken from Swedish massage, which of course I learned with Kroll at The Institute."

As he talks, Max matches actions to his words. Making firm circular motions with the flat of his hand. Covering the whole area of her bottom and nudging her thighs a little further apart as he does so. She feels herself relax as he does it. And then the peculiar sensation as he massages her, softly pinching her flesh between his thumb and forefingers.

"And gentle taps to be begin with." Delivered evenly, cushioned impacts of the palm of his right hand, methodically over the whole area of her arse down to the overhang meeting her upper thighs. "A gradual increase in vigour." Like turning up the volume control of an amplifier. The same methodical coverage but a shade harder. It doesn't really hurt. To Catherine it's like a promise of hurt to come as the intensity builds. And it's as though a switch has been thrown inside her. A direct link created between the action of his hand on her bottom and a twitching excitement between her legs. To her horror she can feel herself leaking wetness and realises that as it soaks through his trouser leg, he can't help but be aware of what he's doing to her.

And now he's smacking down harder on her arse, holding her firmly with his left arm pressing down on her lower back. As his hand rebounds the room echoes with the slapping sound. And now she can really feel it. Is struggling not to cry out as each stroke descends. Biting her lower lip and trying not to sob. Not succeeding entirely in suppressing the tears beginning to trickle down her cheeks. And it stops.

But only so he can run the ledge of his hand down her crease. And test her wetness with his fingers. Wetness he scoops up and uses to anoint her clitoris. Rubbing to make her moan with pleasure. Luring her into a false sense of security before recommencing her punishment. And he's using a cupping motion across the base of her bottom so that each smack is louder still. Cracks of sound accompanied by the wails she can no longer contain. Until finally it is over. The discipline anyway. But he's not entirely finished with her. Her reward, his fingers prodding and stroking her and it only takes seconds before she comes. Red faced and panting across his lap.

He lets her lie across his knees. Lets her body stop shaking. Stops her putting her own hand behind her to feel the damage. The reddening so apparent to the silent observers on the settees. In places there are even clearly demarcated palm prints to be seen. Absolute evidence of his handiwork. And started by the Master, a ripple of applause around the room. "A fine performance." High praise for both of them.

When she can at last lie still, Max reaches down to pick up a small jar from the floor. Unscrews the cap and takes a dollop of the contents to put on her bottom. It's a cool lotion which smells vaguely medicinal. And it feels wonderful to her as he smooths it into her skin with his big hand.

Now it's completely over.

She knows she won't be able to stand up. He realises that too and lowers her onto the rug. Crosses the room to fetch a soft blue blanket left there in readiness by him for the very purpose of preventing her getting cold afterwards. She looks up as he puts it over her curled up body. To her surprise she's alone with Max in the room. And she was so out of it, she wasn't aware of them leaving.

"Where are they?"

His laconic answer. "Playtime." She can only begin to imagine what that means in this house.

It's not late. The whole session has taken less than an hour. Max puts her in the shower but doesn't join her this time. Helps her dress. Escorts her to the front door and then, removing his mask, out onto the street. Eagerly she memorises his face as he hails a taxi for her. More rugged than handsome. Dark hair. Cut close to his head. Strong jawline. Neat ears. He hands her into the taxi. In archaic fashion, bends to kiss her fingers. Undermines the formal effect with a self-mocking grin. Lets go of her hand. Gives her one of the familiar cream envelopes. Slams the door. Waves once. Turns and walks away. Striding in the opposite direction to the way she's going.

19 ~ A MISLAID SUMMONS

Catherine's annoyed with herself for forgetting one thing last night. She'd meant to look for any sign that one of the four Forum members other than Max and the Master might be one of the four suspects from her office. And in the heat of the night's experiences, she completely forgot. But heat is the right word. Her bottom in the long mirror is an even shade of red all over and once again sitting down isn't going to be a bed of roses for her.

It also occurs to her that she's mislaid the envelope Max handed her. She'll have put it down on the side when she got home last night. She hopes. Doesn't think she could have left it in the taxi. Of course having had the summons already, she won't be able to watch her handbag and control the opportunities for anyone to put anything from the Forum in it while she's at work. A chance foregone to narrow down the list of four. A shame about that.

Work has never particularly fascinated Catherine. Engages her enough that she floats through it competently enough. Not enough that she excels at it. And at the moment it seems an increasingly anaemic exercise. She does it, dutifully socialises with friends and maintains her home. But her focus, her real interest is increasingly upon how Wednesday nights leave her feeling. And the time in between sessions with the Forum drags appallingly for her.

The one thing she tries is to discover more about the activities of the Forum. Barbara she knows to be a dead end. Having decided that Catherine would benefit from the attentions of the Forum and made the necessary introductions, Barbara has consistently refused to talk about it. "You'll understand for yourself when you're fully initiated into it. Better you aren't pre-warned what to expect" The line she's sticking to whenever Catherine raises the subject. She sits for hours at the weekend on-line, using different search engines and terms of reference. She can't believe that there can be no trace of them in the virtual world of digital information but if there is, they've made it bloody hard to find. Her frustration grows the more time she spends looking. Eventually she has no more energy and her head's throbbing with an incipient migraine. Better to give up and turn in for the night.

On Sunday she ransacks her flat in an increasingly desperate hunt for the cream envelope Max handed her. She's almost certain she still had it in her hand when she walked in the previous Wednesday night. She vaguely recalls dropping it on the hall table. She finds herself searching the same places several times, unable to accept it isn't there. She doesn't sleep well. And her performance at the office on Monday is distinctly sub-standard.

Comes in from work, a little calmer. If she can't find the summons then the odds are that it'll be the same day, time and place as before and if she's missed any special, preparatory instruction, she'll have to be prepared to own up and make penance as necessary. She shuts the door, hangs her coat up and in kicking off her shoes, catches a glimpse of something out of place. Down at skirting board level, just an edge protruding from behind the hallstand. The corner of a cream envelope. Which has fallen down the back of the unit. How on earth could she have missed that when she was desperately looking for it? The relief is colossal. She stoops to recover it and reads the contents right away. And is shocked to discover how close she came to being more than an hour later than she is required to be. The summons isn't for the usual time but for half past six. Meaning she'll have no option other than to change and go there straight from the office. And hope not to be seen sneaking out dressed in as flimsy a manner as will be required. Such a different look to the smartly orthodox business suit and low-heels she affects for work.

20 ~ THE HORSE

Catherine's offices are usually sparsely occupied after five o'clock. She prays that people will depart on time tonight. Sits twiddling her fingers in front of her computer screen as the building empties. Eventually can't wait any longer for the stragglers to leave. Picks up her tote-bag and raincoat and heads for the ladies' toilets where she plans to change. The cubicles aren't over-large but one of them will have to do.

She hangs her raincoat and bag on the back of the cubicle door. Uses the facilities and grimly sets about complying with how she's been told to prepare. Any excitement that might be there is overlaid by the fear of being caught. And embarrassed. She takes off all her work clothes and stuffs them into the tote-bag. The only thing she puts back on are a brand new, black lace-trimmed suspender belt and a pair of fully-fashioned and seamed Cuban heeled stockings and a pair of black court shoes. The stockings are so fine she fears laddering them as soon as she puts them on, no matter how much care she takes. Over the top she puts on the raincoat and buttons it most of the way up so it covers her bare breasts. Going out in the coat itself is going to look distinctly odd. For a change it's a dry and pleasant evening out there.

Outside the toilets she thinks for a moment about taking the stairs. But it's several floors and if she's spotted that's bound to excite comment. She just has to hope to have the lift and lobby to herself. At first luck is completely on her side. Nobody joins her waiting for the lift and when it arrives it's empty. So far so good. Exiting, she makes a dash for the door. The click of her heels causes the security guard to look up but he doesn't know her to speak to and isn't likely to comment. Especially as she's past him quickly and nearly at the glass doors. One of which opens as she gets there to find Adam on the way in and holding it for her. She brushes past with a quick "Thanks." Scurries away as fast as is commensurate without a complete loss of dignity. She can feel his eyes on the back of her neck following her progress down to the street and into a cab. She can see him standing there watching as the taxi drives past him. He's too far away to really see but she knows all too well the assessing look which comes across his face when he's puzzling over a problem and she imagines that's how he looks now, staring after her.

At least she's got away though. Earlier than she'd feared might be possible. And far better to be too early at the big house than to be late. She settles back against the car's leather upholstery. The pressure of the seatbelt over her breast reminds her that under the raincoat she's as nearly naked as makes no difference and now the balance between nerves and excitement begins to tip and she knows how much she's been looking forward to tonight's adventure.

Deposited on the pavement, she checks her coat hasn't ridden up at the back. Crosses to the door. Rings the bell and is promptly admitted. Inside she doesn't have to sit and wait either. The two dark-clad factotums who put her in the stocks before are already there, putting on her blindfold and hustling her down a flight of stairs, along a stone-flagged corridor and into a part of the building she's never been before. No pleasantries from either of them. Just a muttered observation from one to the other. "Glad she's early. More time for us to play with her."

"Off with the coat." An order reinforced by a tug on her sleeve. Catherine quickly unbuttons it before they get impatient and try to tear it off. Allows one of them to peel it away. Stands there in her shoes and stockings.

"We're going to make a little film now with you as the star. A sort of porno National Velvet. Although you're far too young to remember Elizabeth Taylor. Come over here."

"Wouldn't it be easier if she could see what's what?"

"Yeah, probably."

"Did you have a pony when you were a girl?"

That seems to require an answer. "No."

"That's a shame. Here let's have this off then." The blindfold's taken away and she can see. The rough stone walls, the camera on its tripod and the wooden horse. And it is a near life-size replica of a horse. But on runners.

"That's what you'll be riding in a bit. Let's have some of this in you." Pushes the nozzle of a tube of lubricant into her quim and presses it. A cool liquid ooze fills her. "Now give us your foot." Takes her left foot in his hands and puts it, high heeled shoe and all, into the metal stirrup. "Now swing up and on if you please." Helps by pushing from below until she's up and settling into the leather saddle. Round the other side to sort out the other foot for her. "Now just need to lengthen these a bit. Can you stand in the stirrups? Okay. Too high. Need you a bit lower. Let me sort this." Plays with the leathers until he's satisfied with her stance.

Turns to the other man, the shorter one, idly watching from the corner. "Need your help now. Get her properly on the saddle." The man comes to her right side. Reaches with difficulty to grasp her waist and pull her forward fractionally.

"Hold her there." Bending under the horses belly he fiddles with something. The noise of a ratchet engaging as he winds a handle. As he turns the lever Catherine feels something moving below her. Something blunt-ended rising up with each turn.

"Edge her back a bit." And he comes up clutching the residue of the tube of viscous stuff which he empties over the emergent mushroom between her legs. A perfectly shaped if slightly overlarge phallus. "Right. Get her on it." And she's edged forward with a hand in the small of her back until the lubricated wooden cock-head nudges into her split. "If that's going in, don't let her move." As he winds more, the artificial cock pushes its way further and further into her. Until the sensation is of being almost too full. The one with the lever straightens up to check her distention. Stoops to give it one final turn and lock it off.

"Right. Now your hands." Ties a cord to a wrist. Loops it around the horse's neck and back to the other hand. Tightens it so she's pulled forward and secured in position. Surveys his handiwork. "Yep. That'll do." And to his colleague "Can you sort out the camera?""

A couple more minutes and they're ready. The taller one comes over to hold the horse's head and talk to her. "When I turn this on, the horse is going to start to move and rock on the runners. And you're going to ride it. Well…ride the cock really. You can use the stirrups to raise yourself a bit as you need to but our instructions are to keep the horse running and the camera rolling until you've come twice. So find a rhythm that works for you and make it happen. It won't stop until you do. Okay? Do you understand?"

Catherine nods. Can't trust herself to speak.

"Here we go then."

21 ~ RIDING LESSON

The horse begins to move. In a rhythmic parody of the real thing. A rocking gait and forward lunging action which in turn rattles her body around and grinds her pussy against the hard wooden up-swelling from the saddle. A bone-shaker of a ride until she learns to go with it. To find the timing of its repetitions and convert them into arousal. Beginning to work the cock up and down, adjusting her weight and balance in the stirrups, instead of letting it hammer into her as the motion of the horse tosses her around. It's horribly hard she finds to get consistency but by closing her eyes and alternately gripping and relaxing her thighs, something begins to happen. The artificial lubrication inside her and pooling underneath her on the saddle gets warmer and moving on the cock-head easier as she stretches to accommodate it and to control the manner in which it moves and scrapes against her. And she's panting in her self-induced excitement. Wanting to come not just to survive the horse but for its own sake. Her body demanding the climax that always seems just another penetrative cycle away. Unaware now of anything except the slick hardness of the instrument of her torment and her potential deliverance. No thought of the camera filming her. Nor of the men watching. Only of her journey towards relief. And it's wrenched hard from her wracked body. Calling out. Hoping it'll stop now but knowing full well it won't. The only change is a subtle variation in the cantering motion of the horse, engendered by some use of the controls engendered by the taller of the two attendants but unseen by her.

She rides on. The wooden phallus slicked now with her secretions as well as the original coating of artificial lotion. A monstrously endless series of sliding penetrations of her vagina which she can't begin to regulate effectively in the face of the motions of the beast under her. She's jolted forwards, backwards and from side to side as the cock-head lances her, resisting her efforts to drive herself towards another climax on it.

When her next orgasm finally claims her, it creeps up on her by stealth just as she's despairing of ever reaching release from the horse. A rippling impact which wrenches incoherent mouthings from her of heartfelt thanks to the supreme deity for the blasphemous gift of satisfaction for her body and thus termination of the contract which bound her to ride the horse until her second coming. She slumps across the horse's neck, semi-conscious as the mechanism slows and finally comes to a standstill. Were it not for the cock holding her to the saddle and the bindings fastening her hands in place, she would fall straight off. She's only vaguely aware of being lifted down, carried into a side-room, laid on a couch and left to recover.

22 ~ PRIVATE CINEMA

The cleft of her pussy and her tender internal tissues take almost as long to heal as her seriously punished bottom previously did. Sitting at her desk and trying to work, it throbs relentlessly and she can't stop thinking about the process by which her dual orgasms were drawn out of her by the horse. Strangely the re-imagining is more satisfying than the actuality, which brought serious physical discomfort into play as a tool of enforced satisfaction. Something she finds hard to put into words when called upon to explain herself to the Forum a week after the event.

"It's as though I've forgotten how arduous it was under those conditions on the horse. Once it stopped being sore, all my body seems to remember is the wrenching joy of coming."

"But you would do it again if necessary?"

"If you told me to, I'd have to. If you asked me whether I'd chose to then the answer would be no."

She gets a chuckle from the Master for that. "We have something to show you. It may change your mind. Let's go next door."

Chairs scrape back and Catherine stands too. Helpless, stripped of all her clothes, and in her blindfold. Until she feels a familiar presence beside her, guiding her steps into an adjacent room. There she's gently pressed to sit down and sinks into a low settee. A moment later and Max is sitting there too, seemingly completely relaxed, one arm around her. The murmur of voices and shifting of furniture speak of the other members of the Forum settling down around her and an exaggerated swishing tells of heavy curtains being closed. Only when the room is dark and silent does anything happen. And then it's the unexpected. Max pulls her across his lap, removes the scarf from her eyes and openly kisses her. Startled Catherine jerks around to see what's happening in the room. In the gloom she can make out people occupying two other settees in the room. On one another man and woman are engaged in pretty well the same position she finds herself in with Max. The one difference is that the woman is clothed but the process of changing that is already underway. On the other sofa a woman is enjoying the combined attentions of two men. Nobody seems to be wearing masks but before Catherine's vision adjusts completely, an electronic whirring draws her attention to a screen coming down from the ceiling. On which a film starts to play.

The scene is set inside a stone-walled room viewed alternately from cameras obviously mounted high up in two corners intercut with footage from another camera set at around head height. There's no music and the sound track plays a conversation between two men as they go about their task of securing a nearly naked young woman onto a tall, wooden model horse. Catherine starts as she realises she's watching herself on the big screen in front of them. Starts to re-live the aching moments as the large artificial cock is wound up into her cleft.

It's hard for her to concentrate in the here and now on what she's watching. Max's touch is seeing to that. He's using his thumb to circle around her clit and his fingers to spread, open and play with her pussy. To make matters worse, his left hand isn't exactly inactive. A well-greased finger is stroking and tickling the little rosebud further back between her legs. Which means he can't restrain her from doing whatever she's minded to do in return in the semi-darkness. From undoing the buttons at the crotch of his trousers and taking his hardening cock in hand.

Looking up, Catherine catches glimpses of the frantic young woman riding the horse. Riding the wooden implement rising from the horse's saddle. She can't identify with the distorted mouth, the desperate eyes, the tossing of the woman's head in either agony or ecstasy. Nor with the panned close-ups of the wooden cock sliding in and out of the clearly engorged and reddened labia filling the screen. It's not a Catherine Rei she recognises.

And anyway she has her own distracting excitement to take her attention away from the filmed version of her burgeoning initial orgasm of that night. As Max's clever touches bring her ever closer to the real thing and her own fingers clutch, span and squeeze his aroused penis with no intention of letting it go until he comes as helplessly as he is intent upon making her. Her thumb flicks over the tip of him and his glans responds with an incipient shudder. He's so close. It's literally a toss-up who will finish first. A competitive race neither intends to lose. And neither does. She makes Max spill his load over her fingers at the very instant he drives her over the edge into a loudly unrestrained climax. If she were not in an altered state brought about by a sheer overload of sensation, she would be embarrassed by the thought of making such noises in the company of others. She might also be embarrassed that her release has banished any cognisance of the extent to which her relaxed response to Max's manipulations has allowed his finger to penetrate her anus once more. And thankfully for her at this point she is as yet unaware of the designs he and the Forum might have formulated for the removal of her second virginity.

The film comes to a conclusion but the lights stay down. Others apart from Catherine are exhibiting the sounds of noisy satisfaction with their partners of the evening. Catherine doesn't want to move. Cuddled into Max, holding his spent cock and letting him cradle her body to his chest and caress her breasts, she feels deeply, refreshingly fulfilled. And it's a happiness she's forming a solid intention not to allow to end.

23 ~ THE SHOWER

The next summons is different in several respects. To begin with the obligatory cream envelope is hidden in a larger manila one. Then there's the manner of its delivery. Not pushed through her letterbox, given her by Max or slipped into her handbag. This time the message is left in plain sight in the middle of her desk, in her cubicle at work. It may be marked Private and Confidential but, since she opted to take a day's holiday on Friday to have her hair cut and visit the manicurist and had meetings away from the office on Monday, it could have been lying there for over four days from Thursday night and anybody, thinking it might be important given her absence, might have chosen to open it. Catherine goes cold at the thought of the exposure which could easily have occurred. The date is the next difference. It's for Tuesday instead of Wednesday. And the venue's an unknown address several miles outside the city. Finally the instructions are unusually detailed, giving her directions for rail travel, telling her to bring an overnight bag and enclosing a pair of geisha balls on a string she's to insert into her pussy before setting out. Catherine shudders at the thought of the state in which she'll arrive at her destination having endured an hour or more of the shifting weights rolling the little balls around inside her as she walks and as the train moves. She knows her panties will be saturated and her excitement at fever-pitch. The obvious intention.

That it's the Tuesday means cancelling dinner with her cousin, the only relative with whom she maintains links. And Monica won't be best pleased having made it clear when it was arranged how much she needs to talk to Catherine. As predicted Monica's furious, worsened by Catherine's inability to explain where she's going that's so much more important than a vital catch-up session arranged three weeks ago.

On the Tuesday evening Catherine comes out of the station looking for a taxi only to be accosted by a pleasant, sandy-haired man with a winning smile and the ruddy face of a someone who spends most of his life out of doors. "Would you be Catherine, by any chance?"

"Yes."

"My sister asked me to pick you up. Thought I might've missed you. Would have if you'd been on the earlier train."

"Oh. I hadn't expected to be met."

"My pleasure. I'm Michael by the way. Hop in. " he holds open the passenger door of a low-slung, dark-coloured and old Alfa Romeo. The car, despite its age, considerably at odds with his personal appearance, which is neither overly smart nor particularly fashion-conscious. He picks up her quizzical look. "The car? My personal indulgence. Love speed. Don't get that from a tractor."

"You're a farmer?"

"Yes. We farm." Adding nothing to that bald statement but somehow leaving her with the distinct impression that the concept of farming she envisages may be a dramatic understatement of his work and landholding. In deference to her, he doesn't drive in a rash manner. He ferries her almost sedately along the Hertfordshire lanes towards their destination.

"How do you know my sister?"

"Through..." She stumbles over what to say. "A sort of club."

He doesn't really react to that at all. "I thought it might be something like that."

Catherine wonders if she should ask her next question. Does it despite her reservations. "You know about the Forum then?"

"Not my sort of thing, I'm afraid."

"No."

"Not really. I'm more old-fashioned. One woman for life and all that. Not that I've found her yet. Madeleine and her husband; they have different views on life."

She has no idea what else to say. How to keep the conversation going. Lapses into silence.

"Cheer up. Each to their own, hey?"

"Yes. I suppose so."

He puts a hand on her knee. No hint of suggestion in it at all. Just reassurance. "If you ever need to talk. I'm sure we'll meet again but I'll give you my card when we stop. Sometimes things with Maddie can get a bit intense."

"Thank you...Michael."

"Call me Mike. Most everybody does. I'm not really a Michael sort of person. I don't think. So Mike it is. Are we agreed?"

"Okay."

"And I think you're a Katie really."

"I was when I was at school."

"Well you'll be Katie to me from now on. And does Katie know what she's doing next?"

"No. I suppose that's up to your sister...to Maddie." And she stores the name in her sparsely-furnished mental logbook of facts about the Forum.

"Here we are then." They're pulling in through a set of big white gates into a curved driveway offset to avoid a number of mature trees. At the head of the drive is a large, four-square house built in a creamy coloured stone. "My place. My sister prefers something more modern. She's got the barn conversion over there. I'll drop you outside."

As former barns go, it's massive. With four huge windows running from just above ground level up under the eaves of the frontage. Mike stops the car to let her out beside an equally imposing doorway, the architrave a beautiful beech surround for a thick glass door. "Remember what I said."

"I will. Thank you."

Through the glass she can see straight into the living spaces. A huge island kitchen with dining and sitting areas on each side. The whole thing impressive in both design and execution. Catherine rings the bell a second time as Mike pulls away with a reassuring wave to her.

The woman who comes to open the door is a complete stranger. Not one of the Forum members who've been at her initiation sessions so far at all. She's sure of that. Both of them were brunette. This one's blonde. And even if wigs were involved then, this woman's taller and that can't be faked. In fact, in her heels Maddie must be almost six feet tall. Looms over Catherine. Well-proportioned too. Smiling as she lets her in.

"Welcome, darling. You must be Catherine..." Who nods in assent. "How was your journey? My brother picked you up alright? He's such a sweetie, isn't he? Just don't be deceived by his image. He's nobody's fool. Smart as a box of badgers, we say." Catherine would agree if she could get a word in edge-ways. "And you must be thirsty. Come in. Come in. We'll have a glass of wine and get ready. Let's go straight upstairs."

Upstairs turns out to mean one of the staircases leading to mezzanine floors at either end of the barn. Maddie takes her straight up to a lovely little sitting room where a bottle of wine sits in a chiller on the coffee table alongside two clean glasses. "My bedroom's through there and there's a bathroom so you can freshen up. Here have this." Handing her a glass of crisply cold white wine. "Sit down. Take the weight off your feet for a few minutes. And then get ready."

Maddie's volubility drives Catherine to the other extreme; of near silence in which she lets everything wash over her without feeling any great need to respond. As instructed, she sits down in a comfortable leather tub chair and sips her drink. When her glass is empty, Maddie insists on re-filling it and she lets her do it. When that's gone too Maddie pulls her to her feet and leads her into the bedroom. "Leave your clothes on the bed. We'll get in the shower."

Maddie doesn't mean that as a Royal we. As Catherine peels off her skirt and blouse, docilely doing what she's told, she's astonished to find Maddie following suit. And when they're both naked, Maddie takes her hand again and leads her to the bathroom and into a huge, walk-in shower. Flicks the glazed door closed and before Catherine can react grabs hold of the trailing ribbon and pulls the well-oiled geisha balls out of her quim. "Good?" She doesn't wait for an answer but turns on the water which jets from the ceiling and also from fixtures in the side-walls. Catherine, unready for the first shock of the chill water before it warms, gasps and splutters. And gasps again as Maddie firmly applies a well-soaped sponge across her back, lifts each arm in turn to get to her arm pits and holds her closely to lather her breasts and tummy. She's acutely aware of Maddie's soaking wet body against her own. Maddie's nipples squashed against her back. Maddie's free hand on her hip, not allowing her to move away from this close embrace. Maddie's thigh nudging between her legs.

Still holding Catherine, Maddie re-soaps the sponge and applies it to the lips of her vagina, slowly and deliberately cleansing and rubbing her delicate parts. Then around into the cleft between the cheeks of her bottom. Softly yet forcefully dabbing the soap until it stings her slightly and she winces only for Maddie to pull one of the shower jets out of its wall-mounting to rinse her down. The powerful spray gives Catherine a new problem as Maddie flicks it expertly on and off and around her aroused clit. The tension becoming unbearable. A trembling begins in her knees and climbs up her body until she can feel it in her tummy and up as high as her breasts. The jetting water beats against her in the waves created by the motions of Maddie's wrist. And she's nearly there...dying to come...when it stops.

"Think you're ready now. Stay and do my back." Maddie hands her another sponge. Catherine can hardly see straight let alone concentrate on the service Maddie seems to expect of her but somehow she bathes the woman's body, skating over her protuberant breasts and neatly shaved mound. No wish to linger and Maddie doesn't insist now either. When the shower's done, Maddie wraps Catherine in a massive white bath towel and pats her dry. All brisk attention, not differentiating between any parts of her body. Except for the special care she takes in drying carefully between her legs and down her thighs. Then Maddie dries herself. Equally quickly and efficiently.

"Now we're ready to go down."

"We're not getting dressed?"

"No my beautiful girl, we certainly aren't. Come on. They'll be waiting for us."

Rushing her now. Not giving any time for that last remark to sink in and breed fear. With Catherine's hand between hers. Maddie urges her down the staircase and across to the other side of the barn where the underside of the mezzanine is closed off against prying eyes with folding partitions.

24 ~ FEMALE TORMENTS

Catherine is given no time to assess the scene into which she's transported. Two masked female devils, their breasts and sexes protruding from leather harnesses otherwise covering their torsos, seize her by her arms and hair and propel her several steps until she collides with a wall, scattering whatever implements are hanging upon it, is spun about, blindfolded, spun again until dizzy, and then lashed by her wrists, shoulders, waist, knees and ankles to some form of wooden cross. "Open your mouth." When she doesn't respond quickly enough, it's opened for her and something round is pushed in which depresses her tongue and stops her closing it again. Before she can try to spit it out, it's secured by a strap buckled behind her head and for the first time in her life she finds herself gagged and unable to utter a sound.

Moments later the blindfold is removed and she can see Maddie in the same predicament as herself, fastened tightly to an x-shaped timber frame. Not that she's afforded much time to contemplate anything other than her own fate with one of the devils right in her face. "You're ours now. No Master to save you. No Max to intervene. The question is what am I going to do with you? But I've got some ideas about that."

Something in the woman's grip; twisting in her peripheral vision. A crop. And if she were ungagged...free to speak...able to beg, she'd do it. Plead. *Don't hit me. Please don't.*

But silent entreaties don't work. The demon steps back. Behind her horned mask, she's smiling. An evil little grin. Brandishing the quirt before Catherine's eyes. Showing her what to expect. What's coming. And slashes it down. Twice in quick succession. Across each thigh. An instantaneous blaze of searing heat and pain. "Now we're going to behave, aren't we? You wouldn't want me to use this on your tender little tits. Would you now?" She places the tip of the weapon on Catherine's left breast and uses it to jab her nipple and push it upwards. "No need to answer me in the circumstances. Anyway you'll learn to love the whip. Look at Maddie."

Catherine swivels her gaze in time to see Maddie's head flung back and to hear the ecstatic moan from her un-gagged lips. The cause clearly the other devil's crop, sawing up and down the length of her slit.

"Now if you're going to be a good girl, I'll un-strap you. The cross is a little limiting I find." And matching actions to words, her devil frees Catherine, allowing her to drop to her knees, rubbing her limbs to restore circulation. "Good position. Let me take your gag out too. You're going to need your tongue in a minute." The devil-woman towers over her. The stiletto heels of her studded black leather fetish boots see to that. And Catherine's head is pushed firmly into an expectant crotch. Before her eyes the puffy labia seem to unfurl and the clitoris reddens and stiffens. In readiness for her mouth. "Lick me now." As if there could be any doubt of the horned devil's requirements.

Tentatively Catherine brings her tongue up the full length of the offered slit. It tastes carries an edge of sweetness. Not unpleasant at all. She licks again, taking her cue from the pressure of the hand on the back of her head.

"You are a lovely little sucker. Aren't you?" Adding with a clear note of malice in her voice "And won't Max be surprised at your enthusiasm when he sees the film?" And Catherine finally twigs that it's not just the horse or even tonight that's being recorded for posterity but every interaction she's had with the Forum. All her inquisitions, her spanking and caning and every fuck. Even making love with Max. The one thing she had thought different. Something apart from the controlling influence of the Forum. All a lie.

And a wave of despair sweeps over her. Giving way in the blink of an eye to a burning desire to punish the woman in front of her, the taunting demon in black leather, with the most painfully extreme climax she can inflict with her untried and untested mouth. Attacking her with pursed lips and an over-eager tongue. Fastening, sucker-like, around her clitoris. Exerting pressure. Then licking around it. Sucking as though her very life depends on it. Perhaps it does. Sensing the woman's sudden vulnerability. Feeling the juices trickling down her chin. Kissing and nipping at the reddened little button. Seeing it swelling, the clitoral hood retracting, Her guide the moans and the twitchings of the woman's thighs, gripping and loosening around her face wedged between them. And a shrieked "Oh my God!" Accompanied by a further spurt of wetness. A shuddering tightening of the hands in her hair. A tottering half step backwards, folding at the waist to disengage from Catherine Rei's tormenting cunnilingus. Catherine herself dropping forward, unbalanced, onto all fours. An unhinged animal in heat.

Left like that for several moments as the devil-woman regains her breath and her poise. And then the slim hand cupping her chin. Lifting it to look her in the eye. "Good. Good girl. Now you do deserve your reward." And to her fellow demon, the one Catherine's obliterated completely from her thoughts, the one working Maddie's crucified body into a frenzy. "Help me with her."

Picked up by the two sets of strong arms and placed on her back in a sort of sling, suspended from the ceiling, a soft leather pad supporting her bottom, leather cuffs holding her wrists and buckled straps around her well-spread thighs. Not uncomfortable like the cross. One of the devils giving the contraption a little push so it moves back and forth, for all the world like an oddly appointed child's garden swing.

Catherine Rei, lying back in the sling's embrace doesn't see her devil-woman selecting an instrument of dubious pleasure from the rack on the wall. She greases the conjoined phalluses of the large double-dildo and slides one end of it easily, up to the mid-point, into her own clean-shaven vagina. What Catherine Rei does see coming towards her, with vicious intent, is the bizarre sight of a newly-created she-male, the gnarled and veined up-thrust of an artificial cock rising incongruously from the gap at the top of her legs. She watches its owner smooth more of a jelly-like substance over the tip and as she advances towards Catherine's ideally presented pussy, the artificial thing bobs obscenely before her.

When it touches Catherine, the devil rolls it around against her labia until it seems centred and then pushes smoothly forward. It lances into Catherine like a knife into butter. Its initial coolness, so unlike the warm penetration of a human organ, is what strikes Catherine first. And then the jerking arrhythmia which prevails until the devil gets proper control of it. Easing it more quickly in and out and mashing and grinding the dividing plate between the two halves against Catherine's suffering nubbin. And applying herself assiduously to the task of fucking Catherine harder and harder with it. And be in no doubt that what's happening here is insensate fucking without an ounce of compassion or affection in it. Nothing but a cruelly dispassionate attempt to force Catherine's orgasm as soon as possible on the dildo's thickness. Despite the stuttering shifts as the devil-woman loses any smoothness of motion, it builds regardless. Getting easier as the demon learns to use the swinging action of the sling to pull and push Catherine onto and back off the unnatural cock.

Ultimately it happens for Catherine who comes loudly and at length but not, frustratingly, for her assailant. Bad news for Maddie, still strapped onto her cross. Bending her knees to align the double dildo, glistening with Catherine's secretions, with Maddie's helpless slit, the devil drives her implement into its second victim of the night.

Catherine Rei is taken in turn by Maddie's dispossessed demon. Only her mask is off now, allowing her to loosen her dark tresses and for Catherine to see conclusively that she, at least, isn't Koss or anybody else Catherine knows from work. The woman, smiling, says something reassuring which Catherine doesn't catch and does something to the supporting cables, winding the sling higher into the air so she has no need to stoop awkwardly to nuzzle her nose and lips into the maw which is Catherine's gaping pussy. It's almost too much. Too sensitive to take any more of what's being done to her, no matter how well-intentioned. Wailing as the mouth sucks upon her. and she comes again. An experience almost painful in its intensity. And the rush of fresh juices coats the woman's entire face, providing a sexual glaze as proof of what she's spent the last few minutes doing to her captive prey. Catherine's last conscious recollection is of being roused and removed from the sling. And half carried to bed by her succubus, leaving Maddie still tied to her cross at the mercy of the dissatisfied demon with the protuberant fake cock.

At some time in the night Catherine wakes to find her lover, devoid of all her leather and harnesses, going down on her again. Much more gently this time. It feels wonderful. But before it's done, she falls asleep again all the same.

25 ~ WEDNESDAY WITH MONICA

Unsurprisingly Catherine Rei oversleeps in the morning. Finds herself still abed at gone ten o'clock, cradled in the arms of a formerly masked devil and with no prospect of being at work until the afternoon. Or later still given that the woman, who admits to being called Natalie, has a leg over Catherine's and seems determined to find out where gently rubbing her mound against Catherine's will lead. As it happens, to a floatingly harmonious coming together.

Eventually Catherine knows she has to phone her boss and make the excuses she's been rehearsing in her head. "I'm so sorry. I'll stay late and make the hours up." Makes the call from her mobile and it's answered immediately. Which throws her off-balance because it isn't the expected voice at the other end but Adam's. "He's retiring at the end of the month anyway but he had to go into hospital last night. Didn't you know? I'm acting head of department now." She's missed that in the intra-office news mail. "They'll confirm me in the substantive post at the end of the month. Assuming I don't screw up and the sales figures stay good. So what can I do for you? You're not in the office? I was looking for you earlier."

"Uh...no. Something came up and I'm going to be late in. I don't think there's anything problematic in the diary today and I can do extra hours tonight and tomorrow." Hopes he hasn't caught Natalie's muffled laugh.

"Of course. Are you still out in Hertfordshire?"

An appalled silence How did he know that? I never told him. Or anybody. "...Yes."

"I bumped into your cousin last night and she told me you had an important engagement. I hope it wasn't for a new job. You're not planning to leave us are you?"

"No. No. Nothing like that." Her brain working furiously in a new direction. How does he know Monica?

"Yeah. Well...see you later then. Don't hurry in."

An understanding Adam Jacobs. Even more disturbing for its novelty value.

Catching up at work proves easier than managing to fit in time with her cousin. The one day Monica can do is Wednesday and that's a day Catherine has to keep clear in case she gets a summons from the Forum. And in due course the much-anticipated summons does land on her doorstep. And it's for a Wednesday. But not the coming Wednesday. They've skipped a week to Catherine's annoyance. She has things she wants to say to Max about trust and false impressions and having to mark time doesn't help her mood much. She reinstates Monica in her diary and they meet in a tiny Lebanese cafe near Covent Garden. Somewhere shabbily comfortable Monica knows and likes. And then to cap it all Monica's late, leaving Catherine to sit nursing a glass of wine and brooding for forty minutes before she finally arrives. Swanning in on long legs, not a hair out of place, like minor royalty.

"Hi, Cat. Sorry. Couldn't get away."

Catherine grumpily accepts the apology. And gets settled with a full glass in front of each of them and some food ordered. "So what have you been up to."

"No. You first. You've been elusive for weeks. And completely evasive about where you've been. It's a new man isn't it? Has to be."

"Yes. In a way. But it's complicated." The understatement of the century.

"He's married. Is he?"

"No. Not that I know. Don't think so." But how would she know if Max had a wife and family or not? *Oh God. Not even considered that possibility on top of everything else.* Has to distract Monica? Get her talking about a subject dear to her own heart. Herself. "What about you? Pete and the kids alright?" Meaning the nephew and niece she neglects outrageously and occasionally suffers pangs of guilt about.

And Monica doesn't give a straight answer.

Press a bit harder. "Is something wrong?"

"Well...things are...a bit strained. We agreed to have some time out. Pete's moved in with his brother for a bit."

"It'll sort itself out. You've been together ages. It's probably just a dose of boredom and the strain of having the kids."

"No. They're growing up so we've got more time. And I don't think we even like each other much anymore. No sex. Not in bloody months. Probably over a year now. And I'm sick of it. And I'm sick of him. Anyway I've met somebody else. You know him actually."

And the light dawns belatedly on Catherine. "Oh sod. You're sleeping with my new boss."

"No. I'm seeing Adam Jacobs."

"Monica! They've just made him my boss. You are going to screw me up so badly."

"No I'm not. Anyway he's lovely. And he speaks highly of you."

"If I was as selfish as Adam Jacobs, I'd let you find out what he's really like for yourself while I had a good laugh at your expense. But you're my only family and I can't not warn you. He's trouble."

"He's lovely to me."

"Yeah right. Think we'll have to agree to disagree on that one."

Unsurprisingly the meal's less than comfortable and Catherine's pleased to see the back of Monica and go home. The thought that Adam Jacobs will get to know way too much about her from her cousin and, for all she's been able to narrow it down, may still be tapped into the Forum to boot, makes her feel physically ill. And fifteen clear days between summonses is the final straw.

26 ~ Q&A

Even a fortnight passes in time. Well it does. No contact from her cousin since dinner together, avoiding Adam at work so far as practicable and making herself feel better by investing in yet more new lingerie. For Max. Though she hates him. On bad days. Time finally to dress up. And take that longed for taxi ride.

The line of masked Forum members behind the long table is less intimidating for Catherine than formerly. Somehow the Master has come to inspire her with trust that things will never get too far out of hand. And she may be annoyed with Max but still feels she has two strong allies in the room now in him and in Natalie. Leading to an enhanced confidence in flaunting her skimpily attired body before them all. Tonight it's the sheer gauzy robe over black lingerie and high-heeled boots as instructed and she's positively delighted to be parading into the inquisition chamber to face them. To be sitting once more on the hard wooden chair. And to be answering their questions.

"We want you to tell us about your first full-blown love affair."

"After Stephen?"

"Yes, after Stephen."

Catherine Rei grits her teeth. It has to come out eventually. "His name was Nicholas". Tries to keep it matter of fact but the emotion bursts out. "

He was a bastard who hurt me a lot."

"Emotionally or physically?"

"Both. He liked to have his own way in everything. The only thing he didn't have the guts to do was actual restraint. He knew I was too afraid of what he might do if I let him tie me up. So he never tried that. At first he was so nice. And he always seemed to want to please me. But that didn't last very long; him making sex nice. It wasn't very exciting but it was…good. And I moved in with him after only a month. Didn't really know him. Then things quickly started getting difficult. He didn't want me to go out or see my friends. He wanted me all to himself. Then one day I was dressed to go and see my cousin and he started a row…which escalated and he tore my clothes off. Ripped all the buttons off my jacket. Shredded my knickers. Tore my bra. And he took me right there on the floor. Like the anger and me trying to fight back really turned him on. I suppose he…it was something close to being raped. It hurt. I was very dry and I definitely didn't want him."

"Catherine. It wasn't anything close to rape. It was rape. You were raped. You do know don't you that here you'll never be truly forced to do anything you don't want to do. You remember the safe words don't you? You can stop whenever you want. We'll try to shift your limits but never over-run them. Have you at any time felt impelled to try to stop something happening to you here?"

"A bit on the horse. And with the woman in the devil outfit."

"But you didn't stop it. Why not?"

"Because I wanted to win. To beat them. To beat you at your own game."

"A good answer. And you did win. Didn't you?"

"I think I did."

"You came every time didn't you? Even when you thought you wouldn't."

Catherine doesn't answer. She doesn't need to.

"You've had some recovery time but we spent last week reviewing your case. We've looked at all the evidence of your progress so just a couple of questions. "What would you repeat from choice? And what would you do better if you did it again?"

Pause. For a considered answer. "Whatever you want me to repeat, I'll gladly do again. I'm sure I'd be better at anything second time around. Now the edge of fear's gone for me."

"And do you think you're ready to share that with others? To make them do what you've been made to do. For our pleasure and your own. That's the goal of your initiation."

"Perhaps. In time."

"Good. We don't think you're ready yet either. But you will be. What happened to Nicholas?"

"He got more violent." Much stronger now. Able to say it aloud. "He wanted anal sex. Which I wouldn't do. And he demanded I suck his cock all the time. And I came to loathe the way he looked and how he smelt. And I stopped letting him get anywhere near me. One day I got up the nerve when he was at work to come home early, pack a bag and leave. I never saw him again."

"Will you forbid us those pleasures. If in the giving we pledge to please you too."

"I'll try."

"I think you will. There'll be no constraints on you tonight. Just the blindfold to make things easier for you. You'll kneel down. You'll be free to use your hands and your mouth. You can do whatever you want but your task is simply to bring off each of the four men who'll line up in front of you. Can you do that for us?"

Catherine nods assent. Not only can she do this but the thought of it is very exciting. It's oddly not at all a submissive task for her. As though she's being given both responsibility and control over what happens. She can't wait to hold the first cock in her hands, to trace its length and shape with her fingers and to taste it. And she's desperately curious to know if she'll be able to tell which belongs to the Master and whether she'll be able to distinguish Max from the others.

"Stand up."

The chair's moved out from underneath her.

"Here's your cushion. Kneel down. Right here." And Catherine Rei's carefully positioned on the dais. Ready to perform her evening's service.

27 ~ THE FOUR COCKS

Catherine Rei doesn't have to be told the man is before her. She senses the movement which places him in the right position for her. She's surprised by his nakedness though. She's expected to be unbuttoning his trousers and working her fingers into his underpants to claim his cock. Instead her hands encounter bare skin, the fine hairs around his outer thighs and, moving around him, take possession of the full cheeks of his arse. She mischievously pinches him at the same time nuzzling into him. The cock, rising as she breaths on it, grazes her chin. The one thing she's been concerned about is whether they'll be clean but the first taste is neutral. Slightly salty. Nothing else. A slight shift of her upper body captures it between pursed lips and she runs her tongue lightly over the glans, learning in the process that the first man she's pleasuring isn't Max. This cock is circumcised. No foreskin to peel back. A shame. She rather likes that moment when her mouth bares the glans. Inflicts absolute revelation.

She takes him in hand. Enjoys exploring while her mouth holds him still and stiffly upright. Hairy and large balls. She squeezes them carefully but still elicits a startled gasp from their owner. Moves up to clasp his shaft. Thick but not overlong. Mentally making the comparisons with Max. Stroking him at the same time as softly kissing the tip. Feeling him tremble, his knees giving way slightly. A thought occurs that he's not used to this sort of treatment either. He's too excited already. She wonders how young he might be. She's sure it's not the Master's cock she's been given and she's positive it isn't Max, who she knows will take much more application to bring to fruition.

As she starts to apply suction the young man shivers and he's already so close that adding in a vigorous tug or two between thumb and forefinger is enough to bring a creamy cascade onto her tongue. She's assumed she's expected to swallow it but there's too much and it overspills, slides down the side of her mouth and drops onto her breast, making its way slowly with gravity down the slope of her bra's upper edge until it can fall in little splatters into her cleavage. She's glad of the sensation of the sperm's warmth on her tender flesh. Finds the cooling and contracting effect as it dries carries a sensual charge all of its own. Especially as blindfolded she can't see the droplets for herself.

Not that she has time to contemplate the sensations. There's already a replacement in position. A larger, mushroom-headed cock nudging at her. Almost too big for comfort. The Master this time perhaps. She needs to use both her hands to hold it and caress it, to stop him trying to thrust it deeper into her mouth. Using her fingers and lips and tongue in an effort to find an effective rhythm to bring him off quickly. Not such an easy mark this cock. An older, gnarled and experienced beast. She knows it and works it accordingly, turning her head sideways to make firm little bites across his frenulum, using a harder squeezing motion on the shaft and stroking as firmly as she thinks she can without causing pain. His grunts tell her she's getting somewhere but it takes time. Long moments when she wonders if she's capable of making him come like this. But in the end he does. Taking her by surprise, the part of the cock deep in her mouth suddenly twitching violently and discharging what feels like a small river of come into the back of her throat. Almost choking her until she can push him out of her mouth, swallow hard and take the deep gulp of air she so desperately needs. And without further ado the third cock is in her mouth.

This one's uncircumcised but longer and more slender than Max's cock. It goes deep until she tightens her mouth around it to stop him thrusting like that. Then she works it as she wants to. A thumb tightly tucked under his retracted foreskin and her lips sucking and pulling on him until he too comes like the others before him. More semen dripping down her chin. Tired now. Her jaw tightening. Get this over now. But reviving as she realises this must be Max. And she wants him. Wants him to feel her milking him for her own pleasure. Wants him to want her as much as she's determined to tease him before the other Forum members who must be watching it all.

The last cock is in no hurry. Isn't even immediately erect. Allows her to breath on him and slowly rises to attention so she it is who must set the pace and seize the initiative. So typical of Max to hold back and make her come to him. Let her do all the work of making him excited. Still be in charge in some sense even though he knows he isn't allowed to control things at all. Even to put his hands on her head. She decides what happens and at what speed. With how much firmness. And when he gets to come. She is committed to bringing him to the brink and holding him there, letting his excitement subside just enough so she can bring him back time after time after time, until it causes him such excruciating feelings that he begs her to make him come. That's what she wants now. To hear him crack and plead and every touch is an intended step towards that end. She works his cock with her tongue. Wetting, laving and nibbling him. Kissing down from the cock-head and trying to suckle his testicles, finding them too large to take easily into her mouth so nipping them instead, little bites with her front teeth which draw the first moans from him and she knows she's getting to him now.

And she does exactly as she planned from the start. Gets him to the point where she finds his pre-cum on her tongue and feels the vibrations beginning in the knot of tubes and veins underneath his balls and squeezes tightly at the base of his cock, stopping him coming at all. Allows a moment for his excitement to subside fractionally and re-builds the pressure inside him. Hearing with joy his anguished moans each time he comes close to orgasm and she stops it dead in its tracks, until taking pity at last she allows what till then she's forbidden and for her pains receives a discharge of sweet fluid into her mouth which however avidly she swallows is too much and part of the flood again ends up coating her upper chest.

And she's done it. Catherine hears the door open and close and then without warning her blindfold is snatched away. And she's facing an imperturbable line of fully and immaculately dressed members of the Forum, each with his or her identity protected by the customary masks but she can see that Max and the Master are among them. So it can't have been any of these men who have just experienced her skills. She's been tricked.

28 ~ MAKING LOVE

"Don't laugh at me."

"I wasn't. I'm laughing with you." Max hugging her wet body to his in the shower, having gently soaped and cleansed her of all the physical traces of her evening.

"I really thought I'd be able to tell when it was you. And... I couldn't. I got it completely wrong."

"It's alright."

"No it's not. I should have been able to tell the difference." She's clearly upset. Close to tears. Time for diversionary tactics.

"You mean because you love me so much."

"No." And she punches his upper arm hard. In real temper.

And to make matters worse he grabs both her wrists so she can't do it again and backs her up against the tiled wall to kiss her. With an unconcealed passion. Pulls her down onto the floor and takes her as the water continues to pour down on them. Comes into her so easily. Her body giving the lie to her anger. Finding herself pulling him tighter onto her. Loving his weight flattening her breasts and belly. The heat of his cock inside her frustrated pussy. His lack of self-control as his thrusts get quicker and deeper. Moving his hips in a twisting motion as he pushes inside her. Opening her right up. She's bucking against him now. Trying to get even more of him. And screaming out his name, not knowing she's doing so, as her nails claw into his back and for the first time ever coming simultaneously with the man inside her.

Later, lying on the bed with him and seeing the scratches she's inflicted, she says she's sorry. He says "No need to be. You were magnificently sexy. In fact...". His downward glance is archly significant but she can't help responding. Looking down to see the warning signs of his reviving interest. His cock slowly unfurling, poking up stiffly from his body, angling towards her. Or aiming towards a particular part of her. One of her legs already rests lazily over his thighs. She slides a fraction down the bed until his cock touches her labia. He doesn't move a muscle. She's sopping wet with her juices and his semen and the merest correction of his erection with her fingers enables her to go all the way down onto him. Complete penetration in one simple sliding motion. What follows is slow gentle fucking which turns her stomach over with excitement. Churning her internal muscles into mush. She wants to grip his cock with her pussy but can't make it happen and it isn't the movement of him in and out of her which brings her to her second orgasm but the softly firm action of his fingertips circling, teasing and massaging her clitoris until coming is burningly essential to her continuing sanity.

And later still she realises Max hasn't come again and it's his stiff penis she can feel poking against her thigh. And she sits up and manoeuvres herself down over his stomach until she can finally take him in her mouth as she envisaged doing so many hours ago. And he tastes so completely of the juices of her own body it's like making love to herself as well as to him. Licking around the base of his glans, following the folded creases of his retracted foreskin. Cleaning him with her tongue. And using the gentle biting action she's discovered on his frenulum, where the foreskin is securely knotted to his cock. Driving him into a moaning, hip-shifting completion although with precious little left to trickle out between her lips rather than spurt.

And yet still later, waking, her head on his chest, to find him fast asleep with his arm tight about her shoulder. Wriggling free to pull the duvet over them. And relapsing into the sweet oblivion of satiation.

29 ~ THE FITTING

Early morning light in the room. Both awake. Tired still but intensely content.

"They've officially designated me as your sponsor now."

"What does that mean?" It sounds serious. Like you're responsible for me."

Max nods. "I am indeed. Responsible for the rest of your training, for your happiness; for your behaviour.;

"Am I allowed to ask you something?"

"Yes, you can."

"Who were they? The four men last night. The four anonymous cocks. I thought it'd be the male members of the Forum. Including the Master and you. But it wasn't."

"No. Just acolytes. The Forum is much more than its ruling council. It's a network. And don't ask me to tell you anymore because I can't."

But Catherine can't help chasing up her one real fear. "Are there other members…acolytes…who would know me in real life?"

"I can't tell you that. But if it helps remember this. The Forum is a world apart. Another life. Even if someone did know you outside they can't betray you. The penalty for that is absolute. Expulsion. And once you're steeped in what the Forum does, very few ever want to leave. So the threat of expulsion really works. Does that help?"

"Yes." She doesn't sound that sure.

Catherine keeps the card in the cream envelope Max gives her unopened until the end of the day. When she does examine it, she's surprised by the contents. Not a summons to the big house for the forthcoming week but an appointment for Monday lunchtime 12.30-1.30 pm at an address in Mayfair. Not too far from her offices. No indication of purpose or who's meeting her there. Her mind races through a hundred different potential scenarios. Her favourite that it's a private assignation with Max. The truth is, with the Forum, it could be anything at all.

She takes a taxi and there's no problem finding the address. It's a service flat above a shop in a quiet side street she never knew existed. She's a minute or two early and her attention is caught by the window display below the sign giving the name of the shop as Eulalie. The half manikins display an extraordinary range of lingerie in beautiful materials and vibrant colours. There are no price stickers. These must be luxury purchases aimed at those for whom money is no object. If only. Catherine is almost seething with envy.

She rings the doorbell of the flat, still hoping she'll be seeing Max or even the Master. The click of an electronic latch tells her she can go in and she climbs a nondescript flight of stairs up to the first floor. As she navigates the last turn in the stairwell a door opens on the landing and a little old man steps out to greet her. He's such a benign figure, white-haired, smiling, with arms outstretched, that she's completely disarmed. He seems to her the very epitome of what a charming grandfather should be. "Hello, hello, hello. You must be Catherine. And such a beauty you are. Come in. Come in. My wife's got the kettle on. You'll take tea? Or are you a modern Miss who only drinks coffee. If you are we've only got instant. The granules you know."

"Tea would be lovely." Catherine struggles to get even that brief acceptance in before he's off again.

"You can call me Charlie. And the missus is Katie. And fancy that. You a Katie too. Do you call yourself Katie or is it always Catherine for you?" He doesn't wait for an answer. "Here she is." A silent head pops out around the kitchen door and disappears again. No chance to shake hands. "Two teas please, my darling. Now through here. This is my workshop." And Catherine lands in a wholly different place to anything she might have expected. It's a factory in miniature. A leather-works. Much of the space is taken up with a cutting table, a sewing machine, stools, racks of tools and hanging from the walls, hides and skins dyed in colours which replicate those she's seen in the scanty lace, cotton and nylon products in the window of the shop downstairs. "It's a bit crammed in, I'm afraid. No room to swing a cat. Nowhere to change either. You can get undressed in the bedroom. First on the right as you go out. But let me see your eyes. Yes, I'll find something special for you. Go and pop everything off except your shoes. Although they're not high enough to get a proper idea but never mind."

Bemused, Catherine goes to do as she's been told but she's met in the doorway by Charlie's wife carrying a small tray. Two cups and a plate of biscuits on it.

"My Charlie likes a chocolate digestive and I thought you might too."

"Thank you very much." Catherine takes the tray from her and wonders where to put it down until the distracted old man notices her standing there and pushes things aside to clear a space on the work-table.

"Go on now. We've only got an hour to sort you out. They said you'd have to be back to work."

"Who said?"

"The Master of course. Who else do you think booked you in with us? Undressing, that's what's required so I can take my measurements."

The Catherine Rei of a few weeks ago would have found it excruciatingly difficult, if not impossible, to go into a strange bedroom, remove every stitch of clothing, step back into her shoes and walk back into Charlie's domain. This Catherine does it with near nonchalance. Without apprehension anyway. Steps gracefully across to pick up her cup and take a swig of tea and says, "Where do you want me?"

The old man swivels round. Looks her over with a clear and frank appreciation. "Just stand in the middle there. That'll be fine."

The threatened measurements are many and varied. And after taking each one, he slings his tape-measure over his shoulder and notes his findings on a chart pinned onto a clipboard. Catherine notices that it's a diagrammatic representation of the female anatomy depicted from the front and back and in side profile.

Charlie starts with her height and then her bust, waist and hips but that isn't enough information. He uses a set of callipers to record the precise dimensions of each of her breasts.

She can't help asking "Is there much difference?"

"Not a lot, my dear. They're both beautiful but as you probably already know your right breast is just fractionally bigger than your left one. Nobody else but a pedantic old sod like me would notice." He smiles up at her and without saying another word, cups the larger of her breasts, weighing it in his calloused palm. The look on his face tells her this isn't one of the required measurements. "Perks of the job, Katie" he says. With disarming charm. She can't but forgive him the licence he's taken. Even the last tweak he applies to her nipple before retrieving his tape measure.

He next runs the tape measure underneath her breasts and with a fine felt-tipped pen makes a series of marks under her arms and below her shoulder blades. "Sorry about this. It will wash off, I promise you." He makes detailed measurements between his newly marked points and does the same across her pelvis and behind her hips. He checks the length of her inside leg, uses the callipers again to make detailed observations of her buttocks, makes more marks with the felt-tip at various points on her pelvis and coccyx, takes the tape measure between her legs and looking her squarely in the eye, runs a finger down the full length of her surprisingly moist slit. His cheeky grin is infectious and she smiles back in silent collusion with his pleasure in her body and in his work. Whatever that might be.

She needs to find out. "What are you doing for me? Apart from touching me inappropriately. For which I forgive you entirely."

"Don't you know?"

"Not a clue."

"I'm making you a corset. A padded leather corset to show off your wonderful breasts. In this colour I think." He holds up a complete hide dyed in a stunning violet colour. "Do you want to see what it'll look like when it's finished."

"Oh yes please."

From a deep drawer beneath the cutting table, Charlie takes out a cardboard box and from the nest of tissue paper within, a stunning creation in red leather. "This woman's a bit bigger on top than you. But this shaped edge will support your cleavage. Your nipples on display of course. The lacing down the back. That'll pull you in. Take about three inches off your waistline. The detailing here lets your hips flare out. Gives you that hourglass shape the men all love. We can't help it. Like Pavlov's dogs we are. Give us your body in one of these and a nice pair of stockings and you'll have us hooked for life. There's loops in the lining for detachable suspenders and for a little lace pad to go between your legs when covering ups required. You'll look a treat in yours. I promise you."

"Isn't this going to be awfully expensive?"

"Not your problem. I've been paid up-front. All I need from you is a second fitting in a fortnight's time. Is the Monday okay for you? Same time?"

"Yes of course it is."

30 ~ OPENING UP

Catherine Rei leaves the flat clutching three envelopes. One contains a reminder for her second fitting for the corset, another an appointment with a cobbler, like Charlie a specialist in his field, making unique pairs of shoes, and the third envelope holds a summons to attend before the Forum. Annoyingly it's for the coming Thursday, a day later than Catherine had been hoping. Twenty-four hours longer to have to wait. And she's discovered that with her-found enthusiasm for matters sexual comes a horrible impatience for delay of any kind.

Once the due day and time arrives, she has nothing further to complain about because on arrival she's immediately blindfolded, taken upstairs, stripped naked and handcuffed to the bedframe in a warm room. Beneath her just a mattress protector covered by a sheet. And she's not just left to her own devices. The two fully-dressed acolytes settle onto the bed with her in obedience to their own instructions.

The first thing she experiences are two pairs of massaging hands, moving up and down the length of her body from head to toe but carefully avoiding her breasts and pussy. The caresses become almost hypnotically repetitive and Catherine, without the gift of vision, slides into a daze in which she's not even vaguely aware of anything else. She couldn't say what's specifically happening. Is too distracted by the firm effleurage of her arms and legs to be aware of the gentle manipulation of her feet and of her cuffed hands. Kneading movements over her ribs and hips distract her from the clockwise circular motions of a palm over her stomach. And fingertips stroking her temples add to the relaxing effects of everything else.

Only when she's about as limp as it's possible for a human being to be does the sequence change and firm hands start on her breasts, cupping and rolling them as thumbs work around her stiffening nipples. Simultaneously her legs are parted and a handful of a warm jelly-like substance slathered between them. And tender fingers begin to move teasingly across her mound and down around her pubic lips, circling and pressing, demanding her natural response and distracting attention away from another set of fingers which are stroking the jelly deeper down her crease. The quickening feelings around her nubbin bring a flush to her skin and little gasps to her lips. Moreover they disguise the lightly circling pressure with which a pair of well-oiled fingers are ever so slowly but remorselessly lubricating her tiny rosebud sphincter. She doesn't know or care that just as her labia are peeling back to admit one man's probing fingers, her arsehole is relaxing in an unprecedented manner and it too is experiencing a careful penetration, so artfully performed that the slight discomfort she might otherwise feel is masked totally by the rising levels of her excitement as her sweet cunt opens to allow him, whichever man it is, freer access to the little knot of nerve tissue deep underneath her clitoris, awaiting any attention given it. And she finds the same area being addressed externally and internally, the invasive fingers mimicking those playing around the edges of her nubbin, rubbing and tapping. Until she can't hold back any longer and her unconstrained howl and juddering midriff give away the shattering nature of her orgasm at their hands.

But it doesn't stop. The touches lighten and are less directly focussed than before but they're still happening. And a more sensate Catherine would know that her bottom is now transfixed by the thickness of a thumb, which never stops its lightly persistent movement inside her. There's no sense of urgency from her tormentors as they aim to become the agents of a second and then a third climax for Catherine Rei. And Catherine is too far gone to protest.

31 ~ CONDITIONING

Summonses come faster now. She's required to report to the Forum three times more in the following week. She finds herself handcuffed to the same bed being pleasured in exactly the same way on the Saturday afternoon and again at lunchtime on Monday. She finds having to return to the office and trying to pretend to be working, whilst dealing with the aftermath of two more cold-bloodedly induced orgasms, highly problematic and she can't wait to race home and dive into a hot bath.

If she thinks that the Wednesday night session will be different, she's doomed to disappointment. Not that any sane woman could really describe as disappointing the effect that can be achieved by four sets of fingers and two mouths on a helplessly constrained female body. She's not even aware of the two acolytes wiping down her sweating body and leaving her alone, half asleep and still cuffed to the bedframe.

What awakens her is someone releasing her hands, throwing aside the cuffs, laying his naked body alongside hers and taking her in his arms.

"Max?"

"Who else did you think it would be?"

"Nobody. It had to be you."

"You got anything left for me?"

"Not really. I'm shattered."

"Well we'll see." And as she raise her hands to her face "Keep the scarf on." Leans down to kiss her. Nuzzles at her lips until she opens her mouth to let his tongue slide over hers. Responds. Kisses him back. Rubs noses. Kisses his neck. And he breathes gently onto her ear. Nibbles the lobe until she sighs with pleasure. Has no energy to stop him moving down to her sore nipples. Is grateful for his gentleness. She's not much more than a spectator as his tongue follows a trail across her skin and flicks, snake-like, over her clit. Little sparks of arousal which he fans into life, subtly using his mouth around her groin. And then he touches her still jelly-coated arse-hole. She stiffens in mild alarm. Relaxes again as his mouth re-settles on her nubbin. Circling and suckling her.

"I think it's time."

"For what?"

"To give me your second virginity." And his thumb is pressing on her anus but there's less obvious resistance now. Her condition in the last few sessions has done what was intended. To associate irrevocably in her mind the touching of her bottom with the pleasure emanating from the attentions paid to her clitoris. She doesn't say anything. She's still not sure if she wants it to happen but if it has to then she would want it to be Max.

32 ~ NEW SENSATIONS

She's lying on her side, one knee raised to give unfettered access to his hands between her legs, when he rolls her over onto her back. "Oh I thought it'd be the other way..."

"No. It's easier like this first time. And I want to see your face. Read the signs. If we don't make this good then you'll freeze up and never try it again. And I wouldn't want you to miss out."

Max's hand is stroking her belly. Working down into her groin. Gently caressing the whole of what her cousin, when they were young, once euphemistically called her Mount of Venus. Catherine loves the ambiguity of the name. And she loves him taking the time to play with her. So slowly. So calmly. Building up the shimmering feelings again. His thumb and fingers spanning the whole area from her clitoris to her perineum. Just like the acolytes did. Though it seems different when it's Max's touch. It has an emotional resonance for her that wasn't there before. And a returning dimension of shyness. But what she's scared of is letting him down. Looking silly in his eyes.

He knows what's happening to her and says "It's alright. You're fine. You're lovely." The reassurance she needs to let him continue. Let him circle her lubricated anus, pressing lightly but firmly until, lost in the sensations his fingers are imparting to her throbbing nubbin, she opens for him and his thumb simply pops inside.

She's only vaguely aware of the passage of time. Everything's so prolonged and easy, she finds herself drifting into an altered state. Relaxed totally. Because he repeats the process of insertion several times, always applying more of the cream, she almost misses the shift of his body as he lines up his cock instead and presses it into the void created by the full length of his stubby thumb. If anything it's the deeper penetration that his cock slowly achieves that brings full realisation of what's happening at long last.

Her fear had been of pain. A fear now banished. There is a touch of real discomfort but it passes as he adjusts his position and stops moving into her. Lying now atop her body, he kisses her and moves his hips back and forth to graze her engorged clitoris with his body. She can feel his hairs stroking her as he lifts himself off her a little and then his weight is back, anchoring her to the bed. And the sensations inside her aren't anything she could be afraid of...they're just different. In an interesting way. She has a growing desire to let things happen. To explore this novel reality in Max's arms. Already she knows that what they're doing together won't be a one-off. And as she relaxes still more even the discomfort of his pushing into her recedes and she no longer feels the cramping anxiety of being over-full which dogged her in the first few moments of having him pushing into her rectum.

He says, "Are you alright?" He asks for forms sake. He can see from her facial expressions that she's fine so far. And that he can move a little more. Into and out of her in a rhythmic way, gradually increasing the depth of his strokes. But being careful not to over-do it. Not to fuck her as hard as he'd have no hesitation to do were he in her pussy rather than her arse.

Max rests for a moment. Letting her get used to how his cock feels where it now is. Looks into her eyes. Smiles and starts to kiss her seriously. Opening her mouth to take his tongue. Punctuating each sucking nibble with small movements inside her. Reaching down to rub her nubbin directly with a finger-tip. Imprinting irrevocably in her mind a linkage between the different forms of pleasure he's imposing upon her.

He reaches across to grab the tube of lubricant and spreads a considerable quantity of it between their bodies, spreading a cool slick down from his navel across her pussy, his purpose obvious once he begins to move in her again, his pelvic ridge rubbing over her clitoris, driving her into such a state of distraction that she can no longer really tell where his cock is and her discomfort is long forgotten. And as her excitement grows into an all-consuming fire and she comes, contracting tightly around his cock, she squeezes him into a sudden and unplanned climax, his sperm jetting hotly deep into her bowels.

Much later, still using side to side motions, he extracts himself from her, brings a bowl of warm water from the bathroom, slides a thick white towel beneath her lower body and cleans them both. Only then does he lie down. Take her back into his arms and fall asleep. Catherine, though, lies there wide awake, gazing at the ceiling, enjoying the steady rise and fall of his chest against her and wondering what more there could be to come in the wonderfully perverse situation in which she's freely chosen to place herself.

33 ~ CALCULATIONS

It wouldn't be true to say that Catherine experiences no adverse after-effects from the night before. But she has to admit to herself that her worst fears haven't materialised. She has a slight soreness but nothing more extreme. And to offset her discomfort, the lingering memory of both Max's evident concern for her and the surprising personal outcome from her first encounter with anal sex, as well as a novel sense of herself as an adventuress, unconstrained by the barriers other petty mortals would choose to impose on themselves. Like her cousin for instance. Monica would never be brave enough to try the things she's been willing to attempt. Her competitive streak finds an additional satisfaction in that thought.

All of which means the nudging recollections of her recent activity, whenever she sits down, are mainly positive. So any distraction from her normal daily workload is fleeting. Apart from the occasional bout of daydreams. Her boss is absent; at a two-day conference with Koss. She doesn't read anything into that. Although she wonders if Monica might. After all Koss is, by any impartial standards, a very attractive young woman.

After what she feels is a fairly productive day, Catherine treats herself to a pizza in front of the television in preference to an evening at the gym.

The next cream envelope is on the doormat in the morning for her to contemplate over breakfast. It poses a puzzle for her. It says she has a free choice over what she does next Wednesday evening. And indeed over what she wears. Contemplation of those questions occupies her all day in the office between more urgent tasks. Given a free hand what would she like to be doing with Max and Natalie? Not to mention the Master. Something for Catherine to wrestle with and visualise all weekend.

34 ~ FREE CHOICE

"This is Catherine's evening of Free Choice. It's not a completely unfettered choice. There's a pre-prepared menu and Catherine it's for you to make your selections and our duty to fulfil them."

There's nothing subtle about the card placed in front of Catherine. It reprises much of what's already happened to her with a few new additions. In fact it reads rather like a bizarre list of Cluedo solutions. She can choose from fellatio, full penetration, anal, double penetration, the horse, dildos and toys, spanking, caning, cunnilingus and rimming; in the main chamber, the ante room, the dungeon or the bedroom; with the whole ruling council of the Forum, the Master, the men, the women or a selected group of acolytes. The one choice not on the list is on her own with Max. She doesn't know whether or not to be glad that preference isn't on offer. Deep-down she's almost relieved. And the opportunity to have the Master to herself is highly tempting. To have the chance to find out more about him. The problem is how Max may feel if that's the option she exercises.

She's almost offended that when she announces her selections from the menu, Max, revealing no emotion, simply turns away and takes Natalie by the hand and steers her towards the door with an arm around her waist. Then the green-eyed monster kicks in with a vengeance and in anger the only thing open to her to do is to throw herself head and heart into the choices she's made.

The Master gives her no opportunity to brood. With an arm around her back and the other behind her knees, he sweeps her up and carries her with ease upstairs. Just as Max did a few weeks ago. He's deceptively strong and clinging to him, her arms around his neck, cradled against his chest Catherine's aware of a slightly spicy tang to his skin.

She's chosen the soft option; the bedroom. He carries her in, extends his arms and almost rolls her onto the bed. Scrambles after her. Not letting her get away. Pinning her down with the weight of his body, his knee scissoring her legs apart and his groin pressing hard against her. "You want this?"

"Yes, Master."

He relaxes a shade, sitting up slightly. Reaches down to check her blindfold's securely in place. Pulls her up a little so he can get his hands under her back and unclip the catch of her bra. Flings it aside. Follows it with his cloak. Stands to strip the rest of his clothes off. Comes back to the bed, stooping to pull off her panties and settles down against the headboard, taking her into his arms so he can nuzzle her neck. Progressing to little bites and Catherine knows she'll be carrying visible marks in the morning.

He's not gentle with her at all. He grips her breasts and squeezes them, almost painfully. Pinches her nipples. Runs his hands firmly down the front of her body. Flips her over with careless strength. She's fatally forgotten that at his insistence on her choosing two different options she's opted to be spanked. He hasn't and lays into the globes of her arse bare-handed but with considerable gusto. She cries out. Can't stop herself. The stinging blows are almost too much. And they continue to land on her reddening bottom long after she would wish the experience over. Only when he's happy with the results does the Master switch, using his large hands to part her thighs and open up her swelling labia from behind. She moans then. As much to encourage him as anything. And his response is immediate. The top joints of two forefingers into the top of her pussy, moving apart to stretch her, turning a little to allow access to his thumbs which stroke up and down and then he takes hold of each of her labia, manipulating them in different directions, the surrounding flesh transmitting the sensations along the neural pathways to her clitoris. Wetness beginning to flow which he scoops out and uses to allow his fingertips to glide forcefully around her nubbin. And regardless of whether she's ready for him or not, the Master climbs over her and nudges the not inconsiderable helmet of his thick cock into her from behind. And the process of stretching and opening continues until he can get the whole head inside.

In one smooth persistent push, he makes her take his entire length. She moans again. A different tonality. Trying to tell him to go a little easier. A warning he simply ignores. Moving into and out of her at an increasing pace. Holding her in position with his hands on her hips and his feet now firmly planted on the floor to give him the leverage he needs to drive his cock into her in deepening lunges. Her heads down on her forearms and she's making little continuous sounds. Whether in approval or not he doesn't care. Just ruthlessly determined to make her come in a violent act of appreciation of his willingness to fuck her. As part of her initiation. But mainly for his own selfish pleasure.

And Catherine, becoming determined to hold out against him, is undermined by the dancing rhythm with which he moves, scraping his cock along the uppermost wall of her pussy, occasionally going deep enough to nudge her cervix with his glans. And against her will, Catherine finds herself rapidly shaken by the convulsions of an early and irresistible first climax. Her legs collapse, unable to support her weight and she pulls clear of the Master's marauding cock. Un-phased, he almost picks her up by the ankles to flip her over onto her back. Grabs a pillow, shoves it into place under her arse and sinks straight back into her, missionary style. She's not quite with things now and he's simply rampant, fucking her with all the strength and power he possesses. Only one thing matters to him. The rippling sensations which herald the point of no return. And getting the friction inside the wetness of her gaping pussy to come. And when he does, with a roar of triumph, it rouses Catherine from her near-stupor only to disappoint her expectation of being filled to the brim with his outpourings. He, unlike Max, is wearing a condom inside her.

The one thing Catherine does discover about the Master does nothing to provide any clue to his identity. It's that he has astonishing powers of recovery. Within mere minutes his cock is inside her again and if he's less harsh with her, she pays the price of enduring a much longer session underneath him. And within the hour, after a spell of biting her tender breasts, he's hammering inside her for a third time. And now she's so exhausted there is absolutely no prospect of matching him with a third and final climax.

35 ~ PREPARATIONS

Another week on from her second visit to Charlie Krogel and the little workshop above Eulalie. Time for her third and final fitting. In the interim she's been to the shoemaker and had a last made for each foot. And although they're not ready yet, she knows a wonderful pair of black calf stiletto shoes with delicate ankle straps is being constructed for her.

Charlie's delighted to see her. "Come in sweet thing. You won't be safe today. My wife's gone shopping. And she'll be hours. What will we get up to, heh? Have I done a wonderful job for you. Come and see. You'll love it."

The corset's in one of Charlie's large cardboard boxes in his bedroom ready for her. "I'll need to help you into it." The old man sits down on the end of the bed, with a big smile and glittering eyes, watching her get undressed. Catherine doesn't resent his presumption or his blatant voyeurism. He's not pretending or sneaky like so many men. He wants to see her body, making that obvious, and she sees no reason not to let him. In fact as she disrobes, she puts on a little show to tease him, taking care about how she takes off each garment and peeping provocatively at him from under her eyelashes.

And Charlie sees no reason not to respond with absolute honesty, telling her "You are so beautiful. Here let me open the box for you." He pulls out his handiwork and holds it up. Catherine is amazed. At the colour of it. At the neatness of the contrasting stitching. At the sheer quality of the workmanship. Charlie slackens the lacing at the back and helps her step into it. She pulls it up and holds it in place. The lining is snugly soft and comfortable on her bare skin. Charlie, with a strength which belies his stature, pulls it in tightly into the small of her back and begins the process of tightly lacing the lower half. "Stomach in" he says and pulls tighter still. "Not too uncomfortable?"

"No, it's okay."

"Top half then" and Charlie proceeds with the upper lacing. Pauses to help nestle Catherine's breasts into position, resting comfortably exposed as the corset has been designed to achieve. Finishes the lacing. And expresses his approval with a wolf-whistle.

"Now last touches. Here's the bande." He produces a strip of black lace. "It goes between your legs to cover your sex and fastens to the front and back of the corset with these little buttons." Charlie secures it in position. "Comfortable? Yes?"

"Yes, it is."

"Then there are the suspender straps. They hook on at these four points under the edge of the corset. I've taken the liberty of putting a few packets of stockings from Eulalie in the box so you're all set up. Have a look at yourself in the mirror here. Are you sure nothing needs further adjustment?"

"No. It's wonderful. Now I just need to collect my shoes."

"Actually, there is one more thing. In the wardrobe. The Master sent it." He retrieves a large carrier bag and tips a large black, velvet garment onto the bed. Picks it up and shakes out the creases. Settles the cloak over her shoulders. Does up the clasp at her throat. It's unusual. Someone's idea of a joke. An up-risen silver phallus. Finely detailed. It makes Catherine smile. But the cloak over the corset, even without shoes and stockings, forms a magnificently sensual outfit.

"Let's pack you up then." The reverse process. Removing the cloak. Unlacing and wriggling free of the corset.

Charlie passes Catherine her pink panties and she slips them on. Then her bra. In the middle of fastening it, something wicked occurs to her. "Hold on, Charlie. Something I need to do first. This is a thank you from me." And without further thought she drops to her knees in front of him, her fingers at the old man's crotch, unzipping him and pulling out a very respectable and stiffening cock. To which her lips attach limpet-like. As she sucks he grows harder still and there's nothing old or withered about the organ in her mouth. Nor about the load he spills onto her tongue a few moments later.

And if she was at all concerned that she might have over-excited him, the boyish grin and the jaunty air with which he tucks himself away and re-fastens his trousers, are sufficiently reassuring. "That was…superb. You have a very great talent, my dear. No wonder the Master wishes to invest in you."

"Thank you, Charlie. For everything."

36 ~ THE CHAIR

A break with protocol. On her arrival at seven o'clock sharp, Catherine Rei is shown by the butler, Nero directly into the main hall. It's empty of people but not of furniture. The normal high table is there with its complement of six chairs. So is the dais but her normal straight-backed chair is missing. There's something much more substantial standing there.

"They'll be along for you in a minute, Miss"

"Thank you." She doesn't use the name she's been told in case it's a practical joke being played on her. And if she uses it, he may think she's mocking him.

She takes the time she's been granted to look over the heavy piece of furniture on the dais. It's more like a lolling, oversized tongue than a chair. It has arms but in shape it arches up from the seat and then inclines down to the floor. It's well-padded in worn chestnut leather and the bottom half seems to be made of two conjoined sections. The design could be sixties in conception but the finish seems much older. And when she looks closer the chair possesses unique features. The sort of features she's less likely to miss spotting these days, however well-concealed. There are anchor points, metal rings along each side, tucked underneath the upholstery. And low down on each side underneath the main seat is a rotating handle which must do something although it's not clear what. The other thing she can see is a slightly sinister staining and discolouration of the leather in places.

She turns at the rattle of the door handle and finds herself alone no longer. In the room with her are two male acolytes. Both dressed in black but this time both masked. Devil masks. With horns. They're something of a matched pair for height and weight and the only way she can distinguish one from the other is the differences in their masks. One is a deep shade of crimson, the colour of drying blood, and the other the hue of beaten silver. Crimson-mask is carrying a canvas bag and its contents clink as he moves.

Silver-mask speaks first. "You should be undressed already."

"I'm sorry, I didn't..."

"Just do it."

She obeys as quickly as she can, fearing punishment. Neither man seems overly interested in watching her. One's observing the other bending down to adjust one of the ratcheting handles on the side of the chair.

"Pile up your clothes on the side table over there."

Doing that means scurrying naked past the massive window, hoping nobody's looking up from the pavement outside.

"Now come and sit here. Right in the middle."

The chair is comfortable to lie down on but silver-mask has done something to adjust its angles and now its shape reminds Catherine of something else which she can't quite identify. "Use the armrests." And then it comes to her. It reminds her of a dentist's chair. Except that those don't come with restraints. The straps from the canvas bag. The acolytes are feeding those through the metal rings and using them to secure her in place so she can't move. First her wrists and arms are bound to the arm-rests. Next straps are placed across her body. One passes under her breasts. Another across her hips. Both are pulled tight. Finally her ankles and legs. The straps pass down through the join in the lower part of the chair. Then silver-mask turns the other handle and, with a creaking of timber and leather, what should have been an obvious possibility to Catherine begins to happen. The bottom half cranks into an inverted Y-shape, stretching her legs apart as it does so. Crimson-mask on the other side finishes things off. Turning that handle raises and tilts the chair back until Catherine's head is lower than her hips, an odd sensation when added to the open vulnerability the chair is intended to cause.

The early evening sunlight slanting down into the room alights on Catherine's spread-eagled body but heedless of that crimson-mask turns on the lights. The point of doing so becomes clear when his colleague draws all the curtains. He then crosses to a wall-mounted panel, examines the labels and flicks a switch. A single bright spotlight on a rig mounted from the ceiling comes on. It's beam transfixes Catherine captive on the chair. The other lights are turned off again and the door opens and closes. Catherine can't move her head to see but presumes herself alone again.

She's not alone for long and the six full members of the Forum take their places. It sounds to Catherine as though some form of lottery is taking place. Somebody says, "I've got the Knave." It sounds to her like Max. But another male voice announces that they've trumped him.

"You're first up then." The Master. "Unless anybody's got Kings or Aces?"

"I have." A woman. Sounding pleased. Catherine thinks it could be Natalie.

"Then you're first. Bring a cushion."

A scraping of chairs. And although the spotlight in her eyes stops her seeing them, Catherine's positive that a semi-circle of observers has formed around the foot of her chair.

The first thing Catherine feels is the hint of soft breath across her cleft. If she's right it's Natalie whose fingers are touching her. But then something else traces it's light tickling path from her navel into and around her groin. She's not at all sure what it is. It's certainly inert not human. It feels like hair but somehow more resistant as well as being gentle on her skin. She could get used to this. Whatever it is, its application is interspersed with moist kisses from Natalie's lips. She already feels very relaxed and her slit increasingly damp. Then there's something hard tapping on her clitoris before it's replaced by a dragging, soft twirling around and around. If it continues then Catherine's sure there'll be one inevitable outcome. Instead it takes her to the brink and then stops.

It's replaced by thick fingers parting her labia and a hot tongue plunging into her pussy, accompanied by the rasp of light beard growth on the inside of her well-spread thighs. She figures it must be the body-builder. If it is, he has a surprisingly delicate touch for such a big man. His breath on her and the way he licks into and around her suggests subtlety of purpose and now in her head Catherine wonders what it would be like to have his bulk lying on top of her and wonders what his cock would feel like inside her and whether he'd be as careful with it as he's being with his mouth and hands.

The thought of welcoming this stranger into her body becomes a distant reality as the holder of the Jack of Hearts in the Master's lottery takes over, sliding his cock straight into her over-heated pussy but she recognises it immediately. Its length and fit, its neat, uncircumcised head give it away. It has to be Max. She's certain of it and allows herself small sighs of delight as he works his cock in and out if her, beginning at length to lose control. Fortunately at the same time she does too, coming noisily as he brings himself off in her tight little quim.

She's much looser as the Master takes his turn with her. As before when she chose to have a private session with him, there's less finesse and much harder thrusting to be had from his thickly swollen cock. But those who've gone before have prepared her well and she shrieks through a second stunning climax with him.

It's less easy for her to respond to the cold plastic of Amanda's dildo which she inserts without further lubrication as soon as the Master withdraws. The devil-woman works her with more variation than the other time she's had that phallus inside her. But it takes a long time and fingers softly moving around her nubbin to bring her anywhere near a satisfactory conclusion. What tips her over is Max beside her, whispering in her ear and raising her up at the vital moment. The rush of blood to her head has a devastating power she's never experienced and it finishes her off with a vengeance.

There is of course a sixth Forum member, of slimmer build and slightly inclined towards subservience. Especially where Amanda's concerned and as she pulls out of Catherine's recumbent body, he steps in with a sponge and towel to wipe down the part of the double dildo protruding from the devil-woman's pussy and then to clean Catherine's shaking body too.

She's allowed to lie there a while longer. Nearly asleep, she's dimly aware of Max talking to her in low tones, saying lovely things she's desperate to take in and remember. But after everything she's been through she can't. Much to her own chagrin.

37 ~ HINTS

The atmosphere in the office all week strikes Catherine as odd. Adam exercising his new-found managerial muscle she can understand however irritating she finds it. But currently it comes coupled with a smugly intimate approach towards her which she puts down to his relationship with her cousin and hopefully not because he actually has links with the Forum.

And at various points she bumps into Koss, John and Mitch and they all seem affected in their dealings with her. Or perhaps it's Catherine herself who's on edge with them.

The trouble is that while she's sure that none of them are actual Forum members, since discovering that there are apparently countless acolytes in training, she's realised any or all of them could know full well about her currently unusual sexual status. In fact if she allowed herself to be whole-heartedly paranoid, she could perceive hints in what each and every one of them has to say to her that they know more about her than they should.

Doing anything to actively sound them out seems fraught with danger to Catherine. She's not skilful enough at dissembling to avoid the risk of giving more away than she might learn. The only solution is to keep a weather-eye open in all her dealings with the Forum and to keep building her mental dossier on everything and everyone she meets there. At least once she's worked that out in her head she can relax a little, get her work done and look forward to her next session. And she doesn't have to wait for her summons. It landed on her doormat immediately after her last visit. The only difference between it and previous summonses is that it promises her an unforgettable evening. As if an evening with the Forum could be anything else.

38 ~ AN OFFERED REVENGE

Catherine isn't required to make a formal appearance before the Forum this evening. On arrival she's instructed to take off her clothes, put on a hooded cloak given her by Nero and join a gathering of the Forum's members in a small inner room. There are no seats in the room other than a single chair on a platform. Catherine presumes that to be for her but she's left to stand beside Max while the Master takes the stage to make a solemn pronouncement.

"Every once in a while each member of the Forum; that includes me; must surrender their position and become for the night a mere acolyte, to be commanded, used, punished and pleasured at the will of the ruling council. Tonight, as she knows, it's the turn of…we'll call her A. Does anybody wish to claim the right to rule this woman?"

"I do."

Max's voice. Much to Catherine's shock. *Why would he want her, the Devil-Woman, when he has me?* And she can say nothing. Can't object. Can't question the Master's decision when he says, "So be it."

Max takes the Devil-Woman firmly by the arm. Tells Catherine to follow. Leads the way upstairs to a big bedroom. Tears the big double dildo she's wearing out of her pussy and literally throws the woman onto the bed. Showing what, if Catherine didn't know him better, she might perceive to be anger. More gently positions Catherine on her back with her head towards the foot of the bed.

"Time to make amends, Amanda. You know what you have to do." And without any further instructions the cowed Devil-Woman, who now has a name, crawls over Catherine's body on her hands and knees. Her bottom in the air, her depilated cleft above Catherine's face and her own mouth hovering over Catherine's pussy. "Go on. Show her how sorry you are for the way you treated her." And Amanda's head dips low. Softly blowing breath-warmed air onto Catherine's most sensitive parts before her mouth sinks into contact and she begins to nip and suck, slowly but remorselessly tracking a route which zig-zags across and down until she's covered every little bit of flesh between navel and perineum except, as yet, for her clitoris and labia. That comes next with Catherine, uncomfortable at first, beginning to pant and gasp as her feelings change, threatening to spill out into uncontrolled enthusiasm. It becomes harder to keep still under Amanda's ministrations as tongue, lips and nibbling teeth burrow into her pussy and a neat little nose nudges and slides over Catherine's nubbin, time after time.

Catherine becomes blissfully unaware of anything else as Amanda works on her. As she uses her thumbs to open up the labia so her tongue can get deeper into Catherine. Who's unable to stop herself grunting now. Her head going from side to side as the indulgent pleasure increases. Until two hands still her movements and a naked Max straddles her face, his hardening cock nudging into Catherine's mouth. Her lips and tongue seal willingly around it and now she tries as best she can to focus on him as Amanda carries on her well-practised cunnilingus, trying to drive Catherine over the edge. Max doesn't leave his cock in Catherine's mouth more than a moment or two. Instead he kneels up on the bed to create the correct angle and thrusts savagely into Amanda's untouched slit. Her squeal vibrates over Catherine's clitoris and another renewed bout of licking does it. Starts a rolling climax. And then Catherine's lying there unable to go anywhere, her lower body anchored by Amanda and her gaze locked on the sight of Max's swinging, bouncing bollocks, as he hammers in and out of the Devil-Woman. Sparing her nothing of his ferocious purpose and obviously uncaring as to what she gets out of his penetration, Max races towards his climax. Head back, crying out in triumph as he finally comes. Pulling out of Amanda immediately to let his throbbing cock dip down and unleash his creamy load into

Catherine's waiting mouth. She doesn't even know her lips have parted to take it. Every instinct in her tells her to be furious with him but she isn't. Somehow all the blame rests on Amanda rather than Max, even though she knows he's engineered the whole situation.

The two collapse onto Catherine although Max rolls sideways to take as much weight off her as possible. He takes gasping breaths but gets quickly onto his haunches and shifts off the bed. Pulls Amanda's drained body off Catherine. Dumps her face-down on the bed. "We're not finished with her yet." He takes Catherine's arms and helps her to stand up.

"This woman showed you no mercy. She fucked you with that thing without the Master's authority. For her own pleasure. Not as part of this stage of your initiation. Your job is to punish her. To take your revenge. With this."

Max hands her a vicious looking, short-handled whip.

Catherine looks down at the helpless woman lying on the bed. The hot flush of her anger has gone. Replaced by a colder calculation. She gazes for a moment at the delicious roundness of the up-turned bottom before her. Weighs where the mark of her first stroke should land. And steps forward.

39 ~ FAMILY BUSINESS

Lunch with Monica. Tapas at a bar in town a couple of blocks away from Catherine's office.

"You still seeing Adam?"

"Yes. Why wouldn't I be?"

"No reason."

"You were hoping "

"No. I just want the best for you. And I don't think Adam's it."

"But you only know him from work. Anyway we've been over this before. Let's drop it. What you should do is come over and have a meal with us. Bring your mystery boyfriend. You'll see how different Adam is away from the office. He's really caring. Come on and do it."

"I don't know if Max can...if he'll want to."

"At least he's got a name now." And Catherine realises she's tripped up and allowed her cousin too much information. "So what does Max do?"

What to say to that? The only honest answer would be I don't know and how weak would that sound. "He's in buying and selling. Merchandising. Much like we do."

"So Adam might know him?"

Catherine thinks *Oh God. How do I get out of this hole. I know. Stop digging. But how?* Saying nothing is the safest course.

"Did you hear me? Adam probably knows him."

"Just leave it, Monica. Please. It's all very difficult. When things are easier you'll meet him. Alright? But please don't say anything to Adam. Promise?"

To her relief, Monica's interest subsides and they move onto other, more anodyne, topics of conversation.

40 ~ DAY OF RECKONING

Catherine faces another evening of questioning. Without a blindfold but the Forum sit in their masks in an increasingly familiar routine. And a rather more pointless one from her perspective. She already knows and can identify, masked or not, four of the six members; Amanda, Natalie, Max and the Master. And she can distinguish between the other two based on their sexual preferences. The male who must work a good many hours each week to keep that body-builder physique likes men and the slighter one, she believes to have a submissive streak, seems to hanker after Amanda. Last week his was a belated and unsuccessful second bid for the Devil-Woman after Max had swiftly claimed her.

What she wears is equally customary and increasingly comfortable. The top, skirt, stockings and boots are all black. She's even able to forget for stretches of time that in accordance with instructions she's without panties, her pussy in clear view of the six people behind the table opposite her seat on the dais.

Tonight concentrates on matters of corporal punishment. Starting with the Master asking her "Before you came to us, were you ever beaten before?"

"No. Never."

"Not at school?"

"By your father?"

"No."

The Master lets a brooding silence develop until Catherine can bear it no more and volunteers something more. "My step-brother did spank me a few times. But not very hard. Not like he did." She points at Max, careful not to use his name.

"And you enjoyed that? As foreplay?"

"Yes."

"And nobody else did that for you?"

"No."

"And you came to us and we had you spanked and caned. And then last week something else happened. We gave you a reason to hurt somebody who deserved it. We put a whip in your hand and you weren't particularly merciful. Were you?"

Catherine, reliving the first blows hailing down on Amanda's temptingly presented bottom, has to admit she wasn't.

"In fact you revelled in beating her, didn't you?"

Almost ashamed to admit it, Catherine's voice drops to a near whisper. "Yes. I did."

"And having punished her, did you mean what you said to her afterwards?"

"Yes."

"That you forgave her? Is that forgiveness binding? Is there any lingering resentment for what she did to you? When she took you so thoroughly with that dildo of hers?"

"I feel..." Catherine gropes for the right words. "The slate's clean."

"Good. Then I think we can trust you with another task for us. Another test if you like of how you respond when given power over others. I'd remind you that our rule is based on consent and doing no lasting harm. We have a problem with one of our acolytes who doesn't know his place and has bent if not broken our rules. He has outside this place discussed the identity and our dealings with another person. It seems he knew or suspected that person was an associate of the Forum but he should not have taken that chance. He has confessed his offence and asked for absolution. Which we are minded to grant subject to a suitable punishment. You are to be the instrument of that punishment. Our colleague will accompany you."

At that, it's Amanda who rises from the table, throwing her dark cloak back over her shoulder to reveal a leather harness and high black boots, an outfit with which Catherine is very familiar. She stalks across the room saying only one word when Catherine hesitates. "Come."

Catherine follows Amanda out of the room and in the hallway the butler is lurking. They stop and he hands Amanda a studded black leather mask which she passes directly to Catherine. "Put this on." It fits perfectly without any need for adjustment of the strap which holds it in place.

They head downstairs for the basement and another stone-flagged room, this one containing a large wheel held vertically on a wooden frame. Held facing it and upside down, by straps around his waist, wrists and ankles, is a naked man. Catherine can't help but look his body over, noting his suntan, his broad shoulders, the slight love handles over his hips, the tattoo in the small of his back and his neat little arse. His flaccid cock is largely hidden, squashed between his pelvis and the wheel's spokes but his vulnerable balls are visible and already slightly reddened.

"The beauty of this piece of equipment is that it's gimballed. It's on a fulcrum if that's the right word. It can be spun right round it's central point in three dimensions. Shall we see if he's followed the instructions in his summons and refrained from eating today? If he hasn't this could get pretty messy." Amanda imparts the merest touch to give momentum to the wheel which spins out, down and around, spiralling the man with it. "For obvious reasons we don't gag anyone tied to this frame."

The spinning, rotating wheel loses momentum and as it slows Catherine gets a glimpse of a face she recognises. There's no room for doubt and she can't help the laughter bubbling up. The man she's required to punish is her new boss. Adam Jacobs. An unexpected pleasure indeed.

Amanda stops the wheel with an outstretched hand. Rotates it until it's captive is almost upright. And locks the apparatus in place. "The decreed punishment is a round dozen strokes of the cane." Catherine realises she's talking to Adam when she goes on "I don't want to hear a peep out of you other than this. I want you to acknowledge each stroke. Count them. *Say One. Thank you, Mistress.* And so on. Do you understand me?"

"Yes, Mistress." Adam's voice sounds shaky to Catherine. Understandably so.

"Will you do the honours?" And Amanda hands a thin rattan cane to Catherine. "Warn him you're going to start."

Catherine picks a spot across the fleshiest part of Adam's bottom. "Striking now." She deliberately lowers the tone of her voice a notch so he won't recognise it. It comes out huskily.

The cane swishes and lands just shy of its intended destination, cutting a thin red wheal almost evenly along its complete length. The victim struggles and fails to contain a shriek, gulps hard, riding out the pain. But retains just enough presence of mind to utter the required mantra. "One. Thank you, Mistress."

The temptation to make the next blows harder is tough to resist but somehow Catherine manages it, reining herself in and creating an even pattern, criss-crossing both cheeks and straying across the overhang to stripe Adam's upper thighs into the bargain. To give him his due, Adam, biting his lips, contrives to stay almost silent, a few moans excepted.

After the twelve strokes have been delivered, Amanda says simply "Good one." And steps forward to feel for herself the scored ridges and the heat radiating from Adam's abused flesh. "My turn. It's alright. I've got permission for this as part of his sentence." Catherine watches her spread cream over one end of the long double-headed dildo, with which Catherine has had some close acquaintance herself. Then Amanda lubricates the other end as well as its intended recipient, presses the tip firmly against Adam's anus and commences her irrevocable penetration, moving it in and out of him, opening him up completely until somehow he accommodates the whole thing. From his lack of complaint, Catherine concludes that he may himself have a certain familiarity with the process. She watches fascinated as Amanda builds up her rhythm and eventually can't help herself and burrows down between Adam's body and the wheel, pushing his cock into the space between two of the spokes so she can grip it firmly with both hands, her thumbs behind his glans, and yank it back and forth for the brief seconds it takes him to burst with an almighty groan, spraying hot come up Catherine's arms and slumping, so far as his bonds permit, as Amanda finishes too.

Withdrawing the phallus, Amanda grins at Catherine. "I enjoyed that."

"What do we do now?"

"Nothing. Leave him here. Somebody'll be detailed to release him later. Give him time to reflect on what his sore arse should teach him. I'm getting us both a drink. I think we've earned it." And with Amanda's arm around her shoulder, like bosom friends, they leave the well-punished Adam to his own devices, sore, exhausted and still blindfolded.

41 ~ SMILES AND REFLECTIONS

"Ah! Needed to see you."

Catherine Rei can't help herself. On returning from lunch to find Adam lurking in the corridor near her office cubicle, apparently waiting for her, she issues the invitation she's knows he'll find hardest to accept. "Come and have a seat." A wicked thought behind the polite gesture.

"No... It's alright. Just a quickie." And he blushes slightly at the innuendo.

His unease is something Catherine notes with pleasure. "Well. What was it you wanted?"

"Just the sales figures for last January. There's a query about paid commission."

"They're available on the intra-net."

"Of course. But I knew you'd have a print out."

"Yes. You want it?" Brushes past him to get to her filing cabinet. He flinches. And she notices that too. Gets the file and hands over the copy he needs to see, making sure her fingers make contact with his hand in passing them over. He turns to leave and in her head Catherine lines up to deliver a hard smack to the seat of his immaculately pressed trousers. Yesterday has done wonders for her self-confidence. And the dynamics of the hierarchy at work feel like they've undergone a massive shift. "Hah."

Adam turns back. "Did you say something to me?"

"Nope. Just muttering to myself. Better get on." Almost a bare-faced dismissal of her new boss made in the knowledge that there's no possible come-back he can make. She can hardly stop herself laughing aloud.

It isn't the case that her mood can stay on that elevated high but nevertheless it is much easier now to be around Adam in the office and his wariness of her spills over onto the attitude of others, who are nicer to her, less unnecessarily demanding of her time and, in one case, even offering to fetch her a coffee from the machine. Catherine enjoys the state of play without assuming it will last. That seems to her the sanest approach. Living in the moment. She does wonder though how she'll handle seeing her cousin next time out.

On Friday she's summoned to reception for a courier delivery. The messenger, in unflattering cycle shorts and still wearing his helmet, has a shoulder bag slung across his chest but is carrying the large bouquet of flowers in his hand. "Only from the shop five doors down so I walked. Bit awkward to take them on the bike."

Catherine takes them from him, thanks him, ducks the obvious line of inquiry from Maria, the receptionist and goes in search of something to stand the flowers in until it's time to go home. There's no card with the bouquet so she's at a loss to work out who they're from. Max or even Adam she thinks but it could be someone else entirely. The Master? Her heart beats a little quicker at the thought.

A different courier for her on Monday mid-morning. This time carrying a cream envelope marked private and confidential. It contains her summons for the following Wednesday, describing the session to start at eight o'clock as a review meeting and specifying her normal black outfit but to be worn without panties. Definitely a message from the Master this time.

Tuesday brings yet another package for her. This time a DVD in a plain wrapper. Written on the silver face of the disc is the Alice-In-Wonderland-esque instruction *Watch Me!*

Catherine does exactly as she's told. Goes home after work, makes herself a cup of tea and settles down on the settee to watch the film. After the content becomes clear, she puts it on pause, takes the tea to the kitchen and tips it down the sink and replaces it with the large glass of white wine she needs to try to view dispassionately the video record showing the edited highlights of her weekly attendances before the Forum. If she had believed that having a camera pointed at her when she was straddling the horse was a one-off, the DVD totally disabuses her of that naive notion. Obviously just about everything she has ever done for the Forum's Ruling Council is there for posterity.

Catherine sees herself walking into the ante-chamber for the first time, looking incredibly nervous. Watches Max blindfold her and lead her in to be questioned. The copy DVD has no sound so the samples of her initial interrogation are meaningless except that she can see herself shifting in discomfort on the hard wooden chair each time she has to respond.

She sees herself undressed and tied down on a bed. Sees the men and one of the woman touching her body until the sheets are soaking with her juices. Fingering her to climax.

She sees herself alone with Max. Making love to her. Her joyous response to his hands on her body and his penetration of her eager pussy.

She sees herself placed naked in a set of stocks. Sees the lone man caressing her slit. The ease with which she comes. She sees the cane rising and falling on her behind. Remembers the agonising pain of the stripes inflicted on her. Sees for herself the camera lingering over the marks of her punishment. Watching the film she can recall exactly how much relief she felt afterwards sinking into a soothing bath.

She sees more questioning sessions. Sometimes she seems more confident in them. Sometimes almost panic-stricken at whatever she's being made to tell them.

She sees herself being bathed and then put back to bed by Max again. Watching what they do together is almost more exciting than anything else. Catherine finds her hands are between her legs, touching herself through her dampening knickers.

She sees herself being fucked by the three men taking turns with her. She's now certain, seeing it replayed for her, that it is the Master himself taking her before yielding his place to Max. She watches the Master's cock entering the woman lying beside her just as Max enters her. She thinks it's Natalie. She sees herself coming violently. And Natalie's body writhing beneath the Master. She thinks she should feel a little ashamed of herself, participating in so carefree a manner in such a romping orgy but is surprised because she doesn't feel the slightest trace of guilt. All she can recall is how good it was to be so well-serviced while bearing no responsibility for all that happened that night. And subsequently.

She sees herself draped over Max's lap and him stroking her bottom before spanking her vigorously in front of the other Forum members.

She sees herself riding to consecutive orgasms over the saddle of the wooden horse. And then bizarrely, shot in low-light, she watches herself viewing the same piece of film while cuddled up to Max on a settee. Sees herself stroking his cock while allowing his fingers full access to her pussy. Sees him spurt into the palm of her hand. Watches closely as her fingers scoop his sperm to her lips. Sees his smile as he catches her in the action. And she can almost taste the sweetly salty flavour on her tongue. She can't remember coming again herself. She was so weary by then. But she does recollect the sense she got of being wanted and loved.

She sees Maddie removing the geisha balls from her quim. Remembers how nerve-rackingly exciting it was to travel with them moving inside her body. Sees herself playing in the shower with Maddie. And then Maddie jetting water over her clitoris but cleverly not letting her climax. Moments later strapped to a wooden cross she sees herself being tormented by the woman in a devil mask. Sees herself punished with a crop and then pegged back and forth on the sling by the devil with the strap-on phallus. Sees Natalie eating her out so tenderly afterwards.

She sees herself giving successive blow-jobs, licking and sucking four different cocks for the entertainment of the Forum members. Finds herself carefully observing the differences in size and shape. She's never previously been able to see more than one at a time. Perhaps, she thinks, every young woman should be permitted access to a male locker room to really see and compare the male anatomy and so to better choose, when older, a cock to spend the rest of her life with. And then she smiles to see herself happily sharing a shower and then a bed afterwards with a man whose cock is neither as big nor as thick as some of those she's earlier had between her lips.

She sees her fittings for her beautiful corset. She never spotted the pinhole camera high on the wall in Charlie's workshop. She watches herself suckling Charlie's erect cock.

She sees the Master throwing her down onto a bed, tearing off his clothes and hers. Sees herself sprawling over his lap, spanked at length and then fucked, kneeling up, hard and fast as he comes into her from behind. And then again and again crouched over her exhausted body.

She sees herself lying back in the exhibition chair and all the things they did to, with and for her strapped-down body. She sees Natalie using the feather on her, kissing and sucking her pussy lips and twirling the soft make-up brush over her clitoris. Remembers how wonderful that felt. Then the body-builder kneeling down to pay homage to her pussy but more forcefully, preparing her, as it happens, for Max to penetrate her roughly followed in swift succession by the Master and then Amanda with her favourite dildo. And finally sees the slightly built man cleaning and soothing her with a wash-cloth and sponge, content it seems to serve her needs as she's served those of the others.

She sees Max taking the Devil-Woman and pulling out to come in her mouth. She sees herself given permission to revenge herself on Amanda. Watches herself taking the whip from Max, nerving herself to make the first stroke down onto Amanda's expectant bottom. Flogging her until the tears flow. And finally inserting one half of the double-headed dildo into her own body and using it to fuck Amanda just as Amanda wearing the devil mask had screwed her with it. Remembers how tricky it was to find a rhythm but how much of a sense of power over the woman it gave her.

And in similar vein she sees herself applying the cane to Adam's naked bottom and then briskly tugging a climax from his well-punished body. He came so quickly after being beaten by her. And how that made her feel. Revelling again in having authority over him. Not to mention the sight of Amanda hammering her dildo into Adam.

And at the end of the disc she finds a ten-minute set of edited highlights of all these things. Her penetrations, punishments and climaxes. A myriad reflections on the recent past racing through her head, long after the film's ended. Until she comes on her own fingers, panting and howling like a bitch in heat.

42 ~ REVIEW

Catherine had been right in guessing that the film of her experiences would be viewed by the Forum. She was wrong in her assumption that the showing would be an informal occasion in which she'd be able to lie in Max's arms on a settee as was the case when they watched the recording of her climaxes on the horse's wooden phallus.

On arrival, Nero hands her a mask to wear and insists she puts it on immediately. He hands her a number on a piece of card. It's the number four. And he reminds her not to talk to anybody. She finds out the reason when she's ushered into the ante-chamber to find three others already there, standing and silently waiting. Then two more arrive just after her. In all there are three men and two women other than her. All masked. The men wearing black shirts and trousers but bare-footed. The women dressed like Catherine. Black tops and miniscule skirts, stockings and high-heeled shoes.

About twenty minutes later another masked acolyte enters the room. "Attention please. Line up in front of me in numerical order. Number one at the front. Come on."

The line forms. Two men, one of the women, Catherine, the third man and the last woman bringing up the rear.

"You will enter the chamber in this order and your sponsors are sitting in a line waiting for you. So you will walk until you come to your sponsor's chair. You will bow or curtsey as appropriate and when invited to do so you'll kneel at your sponsor's right-hand. Good. Let's go."

The doors are opened for them and the six of them are paraded into the Forum's presence. The ruling council occupies six easy chairs set out in a row. Beside each of the chairs is a cushion in a different coloured velvet. The cushions correspond with the background colours of the numbered cards carried by each of the acolytes.

The man at the head of the line moves along towards the far end chair and sinks down next his sponsor who Catherine is sure is her Devil-Woman. The others follow suit. The next man bows to Natalie and the woman in front of Catherine settles down beside the Master. Catherine spots her yellow cushion on the floor beside the tall masked figure who has to be Max. She curtseys and hears him say "Sit down, please." She obeys with alacrity, realises she's supposed to kneel and adjusts her position accordingly. Peering past him she watches the last two take their places. A man and a woman for the two other male Forum members.

When they're all in their places, the lights go down and a film show begins, starting with the man who has Amanda, the Devil-Woman, as his sponsor. A few minutes later a heated debate ensues as to whether he's made enough progress to rise up the ranks of the acolytes.

The same sequence of viewing a film and then discussing each trainee happens twice more before Catherine is alerted to her slot by Max sitting bolt upright. She doesn't really watch the filmed highlights of her experiences. She knows only too well from last night just what it is the others are watching on the screen. Instead she examines the masked faces of the Forum members and tries to read any signs of their approval. She can't stand the thought they might fail her. She's not sure if she wants to continue with the Forum but she wants the choice to be her own. Not a consequence of failure. And in the darkness, frustrated by the lack of any clues to what they're thinking, she rises onto her knees to release Max's cock and bends to take it in her mouth. Feels his hand on the back of her head. And his evident enjoyment. "Mmmm."

The sudden silence tells her that her edited highlights are over but when she tries to raise her head. Max holds her in place. With her lips and her tongue on him.

The Master's voice. "Initial thoughts?"

And Catherine has to kneel there, gagged with Max's cock, and listen to their comments and criticisms. It seems to go on for far too long before the Master restores order. "So she's done enough to pass the first stage of her training. Is that unanimous?"

A chorus of murmurs confirms that it is. But rather than let her relax, Max nudges her to carry on sucking him. And the film for the fifth trainee starts to run.

43 ~ DRESSING UP

On the just-in-time principle, a box containing her new, hand-made shoes is couriered to her at the office on the very day she's been summoned to attend the big house for what is described on the note in the ubiquitous cream envelope as her presentation to the Forum.

The summons is in fact distinctly formal in its wording. And it specifies her mode of dress in exacting detail: black hooded cape to be worn over her corset, black stockings and her new black, high-heeled, court shoes.

When she opens the shoe-box in the privacy of her cubicle, just looking at the gorgeous workmanship isn't enough for her. She has to try them on at once. They prove surprisingly comfortable despite the four-inch stiletto heels. So she walks up and down in them a few times, getting the feel of them. Letting her hips sway. Working on her moves.

Typical luck that Adam should choose to walk in at that exact moment. He says nothing. He doesn't need to. Smirks. Swivels. And leaves again.

But even coming off worst in a point-scoring encounter with Adam can't dampen her growing excitement when she starts getting ready for the evening. She's already booked the afternoon off so she can run the gamut of making the absolute best of herself starting with a visit to her regular hairdressers before moving on two hours later to her favourite nail-bar for both a manicure and a pedicure. Then back to her flat.

She forces herself to eat a poached egg on toast and drink a cup of tea. She doesn't really want anything but logic dictates that later on she's going to need the energy only food now can provide.

Then into a hot soak in the bath. Keeping an eye on the time but letting go of all her daily cares and money worries and letting herself be taken over by an ever-growing excitement.

Until finally it's the moment when she must get dried off, do her make-up and go and put on her new outfit. It's laid out ready on her bed. The cloak with the silver pin at the neck. The beautifully worked corset with its suspenders and the black lace bande to go between her legs. The sheer stockings. And on the floor the shoes with the thin little ankle straps.

And only then does an awful thought occur to her. How on earth can she lace up her corset. It took Charlie to do it for her at the fitting. And she's stupidly made no provision for help. Panic setting in. She has to get somebody here and fast. The friend who introduced her to the Forum, Barbara, has been working abroad and isn't back. Monica lives too far out and couldn't possibly reach her in time. And the unanswerable questions she'd ask. There's no other friend or colleague she can call. No choice then. She'll have to put it on when she gets there. Have one of the acolytes or the butler lace her up.

The bell rings. She opens the door still wearing just her dressing gown. And standing on the threshold to her intense relief is Max. "Thought you might need a hand."

All that needs to be said.

44 ~ THE PRESENTATION

The ante-chamber is set out very differently to the waiting room Catherine is used to, as though for a wedding or a college graduation ceremony. All the comfortable chairs have been taken away. Across one end of the room is a low platform carrying a table and three high-backed chairs. The table holds a number of parchment rolls, a carafe of water and three glasses.

In front of the dais is a bank of perhaps twenty hard chairs with standing room behind them already occupied by a group of black-clad acolytes and hangers-on.

The chairs fill up as sponsors bring their chosen trainees in and sit down beside them. The female trainees are all dressed like Catherine, in corsets in some beautiful rainbow hue, in stockings and high heels topped off with velvet cloaks, the hoods pulled up over their heads and their faces masked. The men wear baggy black cotton trousers, chest harnesses and black boots but also hooded cloaks and masks.

A voice bellows from the doorway. "Pray be upstanding."

They all stand for a procession to the front of two men and a woman. All masked. All in black. The man at the back is the Master. They take their seats on the dais, the other man in the middle, the Master on his right hand, the woman on his left. The one in the middle acts as Master of Ceremonies. Neither of the others speaks. From the list in his hand he reads the first name on it and a couple on the front row rise for the younger of the two to receive a scroll, a handshake and an acknowledgement that a stage of training has been passed.

"Who are they all?" asks Catherine in a whisper.

"They're from the Forum's three Chapters. We're not the only one."

"Oh."

And so it goes on. The names announced all derive from the names of Greek, Roman and Egyptian gods and goddesses. Catherine is waiting for Artemisia to be called. When it is, she and Max make their way to the front for her rite of passage.

"Ladies and gentlemen" says the Master of Ceremonies, after honouring the tenth trainee, "We'll now proceed across the hall to the main chamber to join all the others and we'll get the party underway."

45 ~ REWARDS

The party is exactly that. A party. With differences naturally. For starters every guest is wearing a mask. And for those wearing a complete artificial face, the consumption of alcohol requires careful raising and lowering of their disguise.

Even if masks are excepted from consideration, the attire isn't normal party gear either. Far too much flesh on display. The men sometimes still cloaked but almost universally bare-chested. The women encompassing a broader range of fetishistic fantasy. The recently sponsored female acolytes are in their beautifully coloured corsets and stockings. There are three devil-women that Catherine can see but only one equipped with a realistically veined phallus uprising from her loins. She guesses who that must be. Others are wearing leather cat-suits, tight pvc dresses, nurses or school girl outfits with unrealistically short skirts revealing the welted bands of their stocking tops against creamy thighs and to cap it all off Wonder-Woman is here in person and sporting an even more attractive figure than the television original.

There is another unusual aspect less apparent to a casual observer. The possessively proprietorial air with which some hold on to their partners. What might occasionally and fleetingly be the case in an alcohol-fuelled celebration in the real world, more persistently the case here. Masters and mistresses claiming their right in public, whenever they please, to touch in intimate fashion the men and women, some cuffed, chained or wearing leads round their necks, who accompany them.

But it is a proper party. With champagne and nibbles, background music with a beat to which some are already dancing and tight little groups in merry conversation.

Catherine, feeling a trifle insecure, doesn't stray far from the tall and obvious figure of Max, his face concealed behind a gorgeously bejewelled red Venetian mask which covers only his eyes and cheeks.

In a slight reversal of the more obviously possessive attitude of many of the masters and mistresses in the room, it's Catherine who exhibits the greater need for actual contact with her sponsor. And he who tolerates, rather than encourages, her arm round his waist and her palm flat across his tight stomach, as he talks perfectly naturally and calmly to the various Forum members and hangers-on who cross the room to talk to him, unmistakeable, despite his mask, given his height and build. Wickedly as one such, to her, interminable conversation drones on, Catherine allows her hand to travel south, down his torso and to feel him through his trousers. He gives her a look and she desists.

When the man talking to him turns away at last, Max says "I don't mind but you're far too distracting." And then his hand is holding and fondling her buttock. Stroking and kneading it to her self-evident satisfaction.

Concentrating on each other, neither of them is aware of the Master's approach until he coughs, a light clearing of the throat, to announce his presence and says, "A moment please."

Catherine's immediate assumption is that he wants to talk to Max but she hears her sponsor say "Of course. She's all yours." And then the Master has her elbow in his hand and is steering her towards the window, away from the main crush. When they're there he turns her to face him, her back against the wall and his body almost touching hers. Deep inside the normal comfort zone. Then he does touch her. His hand cupping and tilting her chin upwards so she's forced to look directly into the darkly glittering eyes behind his sinister, black hook-nosed mask.

The first thing he says is a warning. "Don't get too comfortable with Max. What you've seen so far is just...an introduction to...possibilities. If you carry on much more will be demanded of you. The journey will take you further than you could possibly envisage. And there is no guarantee that Max will remain as your sponsor. The Forum may decide to change that. I may decide to change that."

"Please..."

"Don't plead your case now. Staying under Max's tutelage will depend totally on the progress you make under his...guidance. So think very hard about coming back to us in the autumn. You show promise but I worry about how tough you really are."

Catherine breaks all the rules then. Feeling it's vital she asks a question in return. "Do you want me to carry on."

And then the Master smiles. Not an openly pleasant smile like Max's but a slightly sardonic twist of his lips. "Of course I do. I can't wait to teach this luscious frame of yours all there is to know." And reaches up, using the fore-finger and thumb of his right hand to grip her left nipple and to squeeze it cruelly. When a tear starts from her eye, he wipes it away with a fingertip and lets her go. The last thing he says is "Make sure you enjoy the party."

She looks round in desperate need of Max but can't see him. She drills through the crowd looking all around for him. Until a gap opens up and she spots him sitting on an easy chair, lolling comfortably, his head cocked to listen to the woman sitting on the padded arm beside him with a neatly manicured hand resting on his leg. A woman in a nurse's costume and white stilettos, the tops of her white stockings casually displayed by a skirt bunched up around her waist, wholly impractical attire for any real medical situation unless the primary requirement were to be elevated male blood pressure. Or making Catherine see red.

She takes a deep breath and stops herself rushing in to elbow the fake nurse aside. Time to be cool. She ensures her smile's in place and forces herself to move sensuously slowly towards him. As she gets close, he sees her coming and smiles. That sweet smile so unlike the

Master's. And she says nothing. Simply settles down on the floor by his side, pulling her legs up underneath herself and resting her head against his thigh. To her intense satisfaction his hand immediately alights on her head and he's stroking her hair. She sighs, the scene with the Master temporarily forgotten.

Eventually the nurse gets to her feet, stoops to kiss Max's cheek and Catherine has him to herself. She would be content now just to sit there at his feet but he has other ideas, pulling her up and onto his lap, kissing her thoroughly, a move of which she avidly approves.

The mood in the chamber is changing. The music is softer, less dance-orientated, encouraging the transition away from vertical expression into actual indulgence in horizontal desire. Max's mouth takes precedence over his hand for Catherine's breast, the edge of his mask pressing into the upper reaches of her cleavage as he suckles her with considerable relish. And the impact on her in front of all these people is extraordinary. As he discovers for himself when his exploring fingers trace their lingering path from enjoyment of her silky nylons, over the bare flesh of her thighs and into her slit which gapes, swollen and wet, before he even touches it for the first time. It's the heady combination of what he's physically doing to her, the hardening lump in his trousers so apparent to her beneath her bottom and the awareness that all around them in the room, other human beings are carelessly indulging themselves in the same pleasures and vices. If she cared to see, Catherine would see multitudinous combinations of heaving bodies, male into female, male into male, female on female, female into male, using every instinct for sexual innovation ever contemplated as possible between consenting adults. She doesn't choose to look up, preferring to lose herself in the feelings Max is imparting. Letting her hand stroke his crotch and unbutton it to extract his fully erect cock. To hold it and squeeze it until Max hauls her upright and swivels her round. Her knees part across his lap and he pulls her down so her pussy engulfs his cock in one brutal sinking movement. And then lets her set the pace of rise and fall on him. Milking him hard. Repeatedly bringing his cock against the front wall of her pussy in a moist scraping which drives her into frenzied shivers of rising excitement. And she can feel his incipient paroxysm and is determined to bring herself off on him before he comes. It's a race with two winners, the contractions of her orgasming pussy around his beautiful cock leading irresistibly to the spurting jets of milky come slamming up onto her cervix as she slumps exhausted onto his chest.

She's only barely aware of being picked up, still impaled, turned about and placed semi-recumbent on the cushion of the chair, Max kneeling in front of her. And then of a still rampant cock deeply transfixing her again. Moving inside her until, against all reasonable expectation, she can feel everything building once more. And between their buffeting bodies, Max's hand playing with her clitoris, cajoling her towards a second wrenching climax which comes before she can believe it's happening. And falls back in the chair, Max still inside her, sliding towards replete unconsciousness.

46 ~ ADVICE

The Forum's dispersed and the house is quiet. She's retrieved her coat from the butler. She still isn't sure of his name. Catherine should go now. She's not sure why she's loitering. She begs to be allowed to sit for a few moments on the sofa at the far end of the hall. Permission comes wordlessly with a nod.

Thoughts are whirling around despite her extreme weariness. Above all she doesn't know if she will lose the nerve to come here after an enforced break. Especially as what is promised if she does is a more extreme experience than anything she's so far undergone.

A brisk clatter of footsteps heralds someone coming down the stairs. At a carefree clip. She looks up to see a familiar figure walking away down the hall.

"Max!"

He turns towards her. "Still here then."

"Sit with me. Can you, Max? Hold me for a bit."

"Of course." His large frame wraps around her, pulling her in against his chest. "What's the matter, girl?"

"I don't know what to do. Whether I can start this again. When the Forum reconvenes in the autumn. I feel really sad. And lost. And I'll miss you so much."

"Well I've got a vested interest. I want you back here. I've got loads more stuff I want to do with you. But this uncertainty is because you're tired."

"Yes I am."

"If you want my advice, you should go and have a holiday. Lie in the sun in your bikini. Recharge your batteries. The intensity of what we do takes so much out of us. We need to stop and have a rest once in a while. The Master's right about that. If you go and sit by the pool or a beach for a fortnight I absolutely guarantee you'll make the right decision."

Catherine sniffs. Considers. "Perhaps you're right. If I come back...I will see you again, won't I?"

"You can bank on it."

"Then I'll try and follow your advice. It's just, Max, that I..."

"Don't say it, girl. Not yet. Now go."

Catherine Rei gets up, crosses the hall, slips the latch on the front door and passes out onto the street. She doesn't look back. Not immediately.

Also by Pete Sears:

The Obedience of Catherine Rei
The Horned God
No Beast
All The Women

Edited by Pete Sears:

Erotic Photography Series 1-62

Coming next:

The Progression of Catherine Rei
The Revelation of Catherine Rei

www.ingramcontent.com/pod-product-compliance
Lightning Source LLC
Chambersburg PA
CBHW050818180626
46814CB00004B/1348